The Tip of the Iceberg

The Tip of the Iceberg

Mary Alice Davies

Copyright © 2022 Mary Alice Davies

The moral right of the author has been asserted.

Apart from any fair dealing for the purposes of research or private study, or criticism or review, as permitted under the Copyright, Designs and Patents Act 1988, this publication may only be reproduced, stored or transmitted, in any form or by any means, with the prior permission in writing of the publishers, or in the case of reprographic reproduction in accordance with the terms of licences issued by the Copyright Licensing Agency. Enquiries concerning reproduction outside those terms should be sent to the publishers.

This is a work of fiction. Names, characters, businesses, places, events and incidents are either the products of the author's imagination or used in a fictitious manner. Any resemblance to actual persons, living or dead, or actual events is purely coincidental.

Matador
Unit E2 Airfield Business Park,
Harrison Road, Market Harborough,
Leicestershire. LE16 7UL
Tel: 0116 2792299
Email: books@troubador.co.uk
Web: www.troubador.co.uk/matador
Twitter: @matadorbooks

ISBN 978 1803133 133

British Library Cataloguing in Publication Data.
A catalogue record for this book is available from the British Library.

Printed and bound in Great Britain by 4edge Limited
Typeset in 11pt Minion Pro by Troubador Publishing Ltd, Leicester, UK

Matador is an imprint of Troubador Publishing Ltd

To Brian Curwain for his help and encouragement.

Contents

The Tip of the Iceberg ?	1
Be Careful What You Wish For	2
Finding the Music	9
The Price of Freedom	17
The Crossing	36
The Truth Trap	47
Never Say Die	55
The Tip of the Iceberg	65

The Tip of the Iceberg ?

Together, politicians and men with international cash,
One wonders what their mission is, it would not be too crass
To suggest that the cash is for access
And that democracy is for sale.
They are all friends together, so it is of no avail
To seek to know what's going on
Whose agenda we will get to see.
We know it's a well-kept secret, at least from you and me.
It's behind closed doors.
Only the tip of the iceberg is what we're allowed to know
While personal power and influence are bought and grow and grow
And the rich get richer.
Decisions that affect us, made without debate.
How do we put a stop to it before it is too late
And the elite rule the earth.

Be Careful What You Wish For

She felt it every time she walked through the "nothing to declare" area at the airport in Alicante, a frisson of fear and excitement, impossible to know which. Impossible to know whether she liked it or hated it. As usual she was met by Peter, who drove her to her villa in a hilly village, a few miles inland.

'What have you got this time, Marion?' he asked.

'Just a few things, but they're good. A small French ceramic and a portrait in oils. I think you'll like them.'

'As long as my clients do. But if they come from a reputable source, I doubt if they care. It's just money laundering for them.'

'I think the Royal Academy is OK, don't you?'

'Even they will have heard of that.'

'I've got a catalogue which proves that they were in a recent collection of French artifacts. I took the photographs myself. It was one of my better commissions.'

Marion opened her old, battered suitcase and removed the ceramic, a pair of boxing hares.

Peter smiled his approval. The next treasure was a portrait of a young boy.

'See what I mean, it's lovely.'

It had been carefully removed from its frame, wrapped in paper and placed between the pages of a book. Even Peter, no connoisseur, could see it was delightful, in perfect condition, the colours bright and the brush strokes delicate.

'Well done, Marion. I'll get a good price for these.'

After Peter had left, taking the artworks with him, Marion made a mug of strong tea. She sat on her terrace and admired the distant views of mountains and sea. She looked at her mobile phone which had bleeped a few times. There were one or two work opportunities coming up which she didn't want to miss out on. There wasn't much else happening in her life. She had expected a bit more from living in London, but she spent most of her evenings slumped in front of the TV with a bottle of wine and some instant food from the supermarket.

Her ex-husband had left her for an old school friend he had tracked down using the internet. They now had two teenage children and were living in Margate. She hadn't been too sad when he left, hoping for better things. But they hadn't turned up. So here she was, over fifty and looking it. Her hair, once a rich auburn, was now streaked with grey and hung like a limp curtain down to her shoulders. All the couch potato evenings had piled on the weight, and she spent most days in baggy brown trousers and loose tops. But if her husband could see her bank balance, he would be wondering if he had made the best choice in leaving her. Her job as a photographer made up for what else was lacking in life. Stealing artwork had happened by chance. She had been approached by a fellow photographer who worked regularly in museums and galleries.

'I've got a proposition for you,' he said, when they were on the third glass of wine.

'I take artworks and sell them in Europe. I need someone who can get them out of the country. Are you interested?'

It was only later she realised that "take" meant "steal". But she was too involved by then. So for two years she had been carrying valuable pieces out of the UK into Europe. It had been suggested, by the group of dealers who ran the business, that she buy her own villa, to give her a reason for regularly going to Alicante where the stuff was passed on to the next person in the chain. The money she was now earning made that easy and she still was able to build up a substantial bank balance. She liked life in Spain, spending more of her time there. She had on a few occasions taken, or rather stolen, a few artworks. The pictures were on the bedroom wall in her villa. She was quite safe. Sadly no one else went in there. Her photographic work meant that she was often down in the storage rooms in museums and art galleries, which gave her the opportunity to take things, but she was careful to steal only small, less well-known art. So, although life wasn't perfect, it wasn't too bad.

From time to time, she met up with the dealers, in a quiet pub or bar. They usually organised it for the late evening. She was given a few days' notice, by text, when required. The underground was busier than she had anticipated, which made her late. They were deep in conversation when she arrived and didn't notice her.

'Marion is one of our best,' she heard someone say. 'She never gets stopped.'

She felt a warm glow to hear this praise.

'That's because she's a drab old woman,' said a young man called Oliver. 'They're invisible.'

There was a ripple of laughter.

'Well, it works anyway,' said another. 'Who cares why?'

She felt as if she had been kicked in the gut but forced herself to stay quiet. She left the room. Outside in the street she allowed her breathing to slow, while she thought about what to do. After some more minutes, she rang one of them to say she had been delayed but would be arriving shortly.

For her second entrance, she made sure they heard her come into the room.

'Hi Marion, let me get you a drink.'

She smiled, accepted, and made a superhuman effort to join in the chat.

'I've got a big job for you coming up, Marion.'

She didn't stay long; smiling was making her face ache and she didn't want to be in the same room as most of them. How dare they talk about her? She realised that it hurt because it was true.

When she got back to her flat in Swiss Cottage, she took a long look at herself in the bathroom mirror. It wasn't a pleasant experience.

'It's going to have to change,' she said to her reflection. 'Starting tomorrow.'

The next morning, she got up early. Her usual fried breakfast was replaced by just a mug of strong tea. There was a distinct lack of healthy food in her fridge, so her first job was food shopping. Rather than driving to the shops, she walked to the local market. Seeing a hair salon, she popped in to make an appointment.

'Just a trim and blow dry?'

'No, I want some highlights and a new sharper cut.' The appointment was made for the following week.

Marion realised that the transformation she was planning would take some time. In the meantime, she would carry on as usual, as far as work was concerned. She found time every day for exercise and observed her body firming up and her weight falling with some satisfaction.

She decided to continue her transformation at her villa in Spain. A few weeks' holiday in the sun might speed up her progress. She declined to do a delivery, saying that she was taking a break but would be available within a few weeks. A suntan helped her look and feel good. By the time she returned to London to her next photographic job, she looked and felt ten years younger. Her hair was short and cut in a sleek new style which made her eyes look enormous. The auburn highlights reminded her of the young Marion when life was in front of her and full of potential. Helped by daily swimming and walking she was lean and fit. For the first time in years, people noticed her, in cafés, in the street. At the British Museum, the curator, a handsome man in his thirties, flirted with her. She thought she would have forgotten how to respond, but she hadn't. Maybe it was like riding a bike, out of practice maybe, but the basic skills still there.

Her next courier delivery was planned for the following weekend. There were more travellers then, so airports were busier, making her job safer. The officials were too harassed to stop and search many people. She had been tasked to deliver a wooden carved icon of Russian origin which had been taken from the British Museum. It wasn't her sort of thing, being heavy and too ornate, but it was probably worth a fortune.

During the flight from Gatwick, she sat next to a man, about her own age. They struck up a conversation and even treated themselves to a gin and tonic. He offered to drive her to her villa. She refused, saying that she was being met and driven by her usual taxi driver. But they exchanged mobile numbers. By the time they disembarked, Marion was on a high. It looked as if her life in Spain was about to take a turn for the better. Her new man friend had an apartment in Alicante overlooking the sea, and they had agreed to meet up soon.

She sparkled with energy, delighted at being noticed, especially by men. She had forgotten how intoxicating the attention was. She smiled at the men, one or two in uniform, standing at the exit of the customs area. They mostly smiled back except for one, who moved swiftly towards her and said quietly, looking her in the eye, 'Please come with me. I need to examine your luggage.'

Marion had a sinking feeling as she followed him into a room in which there were large tables and a few men opening suitcases. She had never noticed the room on her many trips through the airport. She smiled at the man and opened her eyes wide to gaze at him. But it made no difference. He asked her for the key to open her small, elegant leather suitcase. She had bought it in Regent Street along with her new clothes and shoes. There was a matching shoulder bag, which she opened to get the key. The clothes and luggage had cost a shocking amount of money and she felt a small thrill to be seen to own such luxury stuff. The icon was wrapped in a soft cloth and buried in her clothes. As she saw the man rifle through them, she enjoyed their effect on him. He seized on the icon with quiet satisfaction.

'I need to ask you some questions. We'll go to the interviewing room.'

He spoke excellent English. There was no point in denying the fact of the icon. A quick computer search revealed what it was, its value and that it was from the British Museum.

She knew that she would be spending some time in a Spanish jail and wondered if her new friend would pay her a visit, but she couldn't contact him as they had confiscated her mobile phone.

'We have known for some time that stolen artifacts have been brought into Europe through Alicante. You might help yourself if you gave us information about your contacts, in England and here in Spain.'

She thought about it.

'I don't know the names of anyone here in Spain,' she lied.

'In England?'

'Let me think. Mostly there were no names, just one man. He's young. He's called Oliver.'

She gave them the name of the man who had laughed and said that she was invisible.

On the way to the police cell, she asked herself if it had been worth it. If she had stayed drab and invisible, she would be in her villa now, enjoying a mug of strong tea. She glanced down at her hand and admired the emerald ring and her bright red shiny nail polish. A smile danced around her mouth. She thought it probably was.

Finding the Music

He noticed her looking at his shoes. Not surprising, since they were made, by hand, of soft dark brown leather and had cost more than a month's wages, much to his sister's scorn.

'Ridiculous, who do you think you are?' she had teased him.

'Well, I can't go to the Festival Hall in my working boots, can I?'

The visit to the Festival Hall had been long in planning and the shoes were part of it. They weren't even comfortable, but in his eyes, they had shifted him from being just a Welsh miner, to a lover of Mahler, fit to be in the audience. The first half of the concert had more than lived up to his expectations. The stirring music was only part of the pleasure. The huge auditorium, simple and beautiful, the people in the audience, dressed up and comfortable in their surroundings, and the sense of being part of something extraordinary, brought tears to his eyes. He was glad that the lights had been dimmed.

At the interval, he streamed out with everyone else, to the bar in the foyer. He wasn't confident enough to order a drink, so he stood away from the bar and looked around. A woman nearby was sipping from a glass of wine. She looked down at his shoes and smiled up at him.

'Are you enjoying it?' she asked.

'Very much indeed, and you?'

'Yes, I come to a concert at least once a month.'

'This is my first time, and I hope it won't be my last,' he said. 'My name is Tom, by the way.'

He held out his hand.

'Pleased to meet you, Tom,' she said as they shook hands. 'I'm Julie.'

She noticed that although clean, his hands were hard and there were faint traces of black around the nails. His suit wasn't in the same quality league as the shoes; it was rather too shiny.

After what seemed to Tom just moments into their friendly chat, the bell rang to indicate that the audience should return to their seats.

'Fancy meeting up after the concert ends?' she asked.

He nodded his acceptance.

To his relief the concert finished on time, and he rushed out into the foyer to meet Julie.

'I know where we can get a drink, just a walk away,' she said, and led him out into the cool night air. They walked along the embankment and Tom felt his heart swell as he looked across the river towards the Houses of Parliament. This was where important stuff happened. The pub was quiet and after ordering their drinks at the bar, they sat in a corner, close together.

'I can tell you're from Wales,' she said. 'I just love your voice, it's deep and strong.'

Tom smiled. 'Well, I'm not Richard Burton, but thank you. Do you live in London?'

'Yes, I'm an art student. I want to be a painter. My parents aren't too keen, but they haven't stood in my way, so I can't complain. What do you do, Tom?'

'I work down the pit, like my dad did.'

'What about your family, are you married?'

'No, I haven't got around to that. I live with my younger brother, Stan, and two sisters. The older one looks after us all.'

Tom was enjoying himself more than he ever had. He almost lost track of the time until he heard the publican call for last orders.

'I have to go, Julie, or I'll miss my train.'

'Let me give you my phone number,' she said. 'Please let me know when you plan to come to another concert. I'd like to see you again.'

He caught the last train with only minutes to spare. It was almost empty, and he settled down to mull over the evening. His feet were killing him, because of the shoes. He hadn't noticed it before, he had been too engrossed in the glimpse of a different life.

*

During the following weeks he went about his life as if in a dream, He checked out the Festival Hall concert dates in the Sunday papers. He fancied some Mozart piano concertos and started to plan. When he had made sure that he could be free on the day, he walked down to the telephone box at the end of the street and phoned Julie.

'If I came to the Mozart concert, would you be going?' he asked.

'I'll make sure I do, Tom.'

'What's up with you, Tom?' said his sister the next day.

'What do you mean?'

'You've got this funny look on your face, and you keep humming bits of music.'

'Just getting myself in the right mood for my next visit to London. Don't give me that old-fashioned look. I like music, that's all. What's wrong with that?'

His sister just smiled.

'Let me iron your shirt for you this time. You want to look the part, don't you?'

He had mentioned to his workmates that he had been to a concert at the Festival Hall. One of them hadn't even heard of it and they were all mystified at his interest in posh music, as they called it.

'I think there might be a bit a female interest, don't you?' one of them teased.

*

He had arranged to meet Julie at five o'clock, but he got to the South Bank an hour early so that he could walk along the Embankment, admire the wonderful architecture of the Houses of Parliament and look forward to the evening. He wondered whether he had overestimated Julie's attractiveness, but when she arrived, smiling, he thought that, on the contrary, he had underestimated how pretty and unusual she was. She was wearing a short skirt and a tight high-necked sweater. Her dark hair swung in a long straight bob around her face. They had managed to book seats next to one another and during the first half of the concert, Tom was aware of her arm next to his on the armrest between them. During the interval, they walked outside, looking at the river and holding hands.

'How about coming back to my flat for a drink after the concert?' said Julie.

Tom just nodded, too overwhelmed to speak.

Julie had a flat in a large Victorian house in South Kensington. It was near to Chelsea, she said, where she was at art school. The flat was just one big room on the first floor overlooking gardens. Tom had never seen anything like it, not even in films. Her finished and unfinished paintings were everywhere, leaning against walls with one on an easel near a large window. Julie produced a bottle of red wine and two tumblers and poured them each a large glass. It seemed that they both needed some Dutch courage. She lit a candle that had been put into the neck of a bottle and turned off the light and started to undress. Tom watched as she got down to her underwear and slipped into bed. Her smile was the invitation and he undressed and got into bed with her. His physical job had made him strong and hard, and her painting of life models enabled her to appreciate his work-honed body.

'You're beautiful, Tom. I'd like to paint you. The whole class would like to paint you.' She laughed. 'How do you fancy being a model?'

He didn't answer, because he had begun to kiss her, and words were unnecessary.

When Tom woke up, the candle had spluttered, gone out and wax spattered the table. He could see from the light in the room that it was nearly daylight, so he would not be able to get back in time and would miss the morning shift. Julie was sleeping next to him, her dark hair spread over the pillow. His stirring woke her, and she opened her eyes. For a second, she was surprised to see him, and then she smiled and rolled towards him.

'Good morning, Tom. Are you OK?'

'Need you ask? It was wonderful.'

'I'll get you some breakfast.'

'I don't think I've got time. I should be getting back. I've missed my shift as it is.'

'When can you come up again? Soon, I hope.'

'As soon as I can, you bet.'

On the train home, Tom tried to make sense of his feelings. What had happened was like a dream from which he didn't want to wake up. He realised that such dreams can be the precursor to plans. This made him smile. He didn't have to work down the pit.

I'm young and strong, he thought. *There must be jobs that I can do in London.*

By the time the train arrived at his home station, he had made up his mind. It would take time, he knew that, but he had been shown a way of living a different life. He walked slowly up the steep hill towards his house, deep in thought.

'Tom, I'm so glad to see you. I thought you were on the early shift today. Thank God you weren't,' said one of his neighbours. He touched him on the arm.

Tom dragged himself out of his dreams.

'Yes, right,' he said, and carried on walking.

As he continued up the hill, he started to be aware that people were looking at him. For a moment he thought that they knew about his night of passion with Julie and were judging him.

Whatever the reason, he started to feel uncomfortable.

I'll be glad to get home, he thought.

When he got to his house, there were neighbours standing outside and in small clusters outside a few other houses. They stood aside in silence to let him get to the door. When he opened it, he could hear crying and sobbing. His sisters were being comforted by neighbours.

'Thank God you're here, Tom,' said his older sister. 'There's been an explosion in the pit. We don't know if Stan is all right. They are still working to find any survivors. It looks bad.'

Tom felt as if he had been punched in the solar plexus. He felt faint and clung on to the back of a chair.

The next twenty-four hours were the longest and the worst of his life. Fifteen men were killed in the explosion, including his brother and two of his friends and workmates. He couldn't hold back his tears, crying for the loss of his brother and friends.

Over the next days and weeks, the small mining town was overwhelmed by the press and charity workers, as the full extent of the disaster unfolded. Tom went through the motions, but was stunned by grief. It wasn't only grief that kept him awake at night. He felt guilty. He should have been down there with his brother and friends. Thank God no one knew where he had been and what he was doing, while they were dying underground. He wondered if Julie knew of the disaster. It was all over the national news, so it was impossible not to be aware of it.

There was no going to the pit; the explosion and its cause were being investigated. It would be some weeks before the pit could be worked again. Time hung like a dark cloud around him. When he was in the bedroom he had shared with Stan, he was blasted by unhappiness and spent hours with his head under the pillows to muffle the sounds of his sobbing. More than ever, he wanted a different life, the one that he had started to make plans for. The neighbours were being kind and were often in the house.

'Thank God you were spared, Tom,' said one. 'You're the main breadwinner now.'

He had tried to force the thought from him. It had crept into his mind when he learnt that his brother had been killed. He took his responsibility seriously. He knew that his sobbing had not just been about Stan and his friends but about himself and the death of a dream.

It was his day off from the reopened pit and he slept late. He was woken by his sister calling up the stairs, 'Tom, there's a woman called Julie here to see you. It's time to get up.'

She met him with a hug at the bottom of the stairs.

'We don't need the Festival Hall. I've brought some music to you and isn't Wales the land of song?' she said.

He thought her voice was the most beautiful music he had ever heard.

The Price of Freedom

'Simone, you can't keep on about the oppression of women. This is the 21st century.'

'I know that. So what? It's still an issue.'

She sat up even more erect in her seat, her cheeks flushed as she glared at him. He seemed to shrink down into his seat and turned away to look out of the window.

They made a striking couple, arguing in French, seemingly oblivious to the other passengers on the Eurostar train to London.

'Jean Paul, you know how much this means to me. I mustn't miss this opportunity.'

He squinted at her through his thick spectacles.

'Yes, OK. Your book has been updated, so you will have this chance to get it out there, again.'

She smiled and touched his arm.

'You know that you are the main attraction, you're the philosopher of our generation.'

'And you are the feminist, the first and the best. Shall I get us a drink, to help us relax? It's going to be a busy time. Conferences exhaust me.'

He got up. He was short and sturdy, not physically attractive, but despite his appearance he had a sort of magnetism that drew glances as he walked along the train.

The train arrived into Kings Cross station only half an hour late. The rush hour was long over, and they got a black cab to the flat which they had been loaned in St. John's Wood.

'I love these old townhouses,' said Simone.

They opened the shiny black front door. Their flat was on the fifth floor.

'There's no lift,' said Jean Paul.

'We could both do with the exercise,' said Simone, as they slowly climbed the rather narrow steep stairs to their flat. They looked around with satisfaction, admiring the view onto the gardens at the back of the terrace.

'Let's go out and find a restaurant,' said Simone.

'This isn't Paris; we might have to make do with a pub.'

In the pub, which was only a few minutes away, the talk was of the coronavirus and what might happen next.

'I hope it doesn't affect the conference,' said Jean Paul. 'It's taken months to organise it.'

'I expect it will be fine, there's too much at stake to cancel it. I've been looking forward to spending spring in London for years. This conference gives me an excuse.'

The next morning, after breakfast at a nearby café, they each settled down to their work, writing. Simone's agent called to arrange to meet for a coffee and discuss last-minute arrangements. Jean Paul decided to spend the day in the British Library, doing research on some rare philosophy books.

'I'll see you later, Simone. Don't forget that we have dinner with my agent this evening. He's a bit of a foodie, so it might be good.'

London seemed quieter than Simone had expected. The

café in a bookshop on the Charing Cross Road didn't have the usual crowded buzz.

'It's the coronavirus,' said Rebecca, her agent. 'It's spooking some people.'

'Might it affect the conference?'

'Things are carrying on at the moment, so we should be all right. I've arranged for copies of your updated book, *Still the Second Sex*, to be available at the conference for a signing. Should do well, there's a lot of interest in it.'

They discussed their final arrangements.

'See you at the conference,' said Rebecca. 'Look forward to it.'

Back at the flat, Jean Paul agreed that things didn't seem normal.

'It was very quiet,' he said. 'Not quiet because it's a library. There was just no one around.'

That evening, over dinner in a restaurant at the top of a glass skyscraper, Damien had his own ideas about the effect of the coronavirus.

'I've got some friends in government who think we should go into lockdown,' he said. 'If we do, you can forget the conference and most of the other events I've organised for you.'

The thought hung over them and spoiled their enjoyment of the excellent food.

'It means that we can't always have control over our lives, Simone,' he said with a smile to take the sting out of his comment.

Back in the flat, they poured glasses of wine and reflected on their day.

'We'll just have to make the best of it,' they agreed.

Three days before the conference was due to happen, it was cancelled, as the country went into lockdown. For a couple whose lives had revolved around the idea of personal freedom, the restrictions were like a body blow. The British Library, along with most other cultural venues, was closed and, like the rest of the population, they had to find ways of living with the restrictions. Although they had spent many years together, being in the same small flat, day after day felt stifling. After a few weeks they began to yearn for their bohemian life in Paris, the cafés, the conversations with friends, swapping ideas and theories.

'It's certainly a challenge, this lockdown,' said Simone.

'What, in particular?'

'Just having enough personal space. I think I'll take a walk. I need some fresh air and exercise.'

So every morning she set out with coffee in a flask and a book to read. She walked to Primrose Hill, where she found a seat to sit on, despite lockdown rules, and looked down at the view over London. She could see in the distance, hundreds of cranes, signs of the massive development taking place, now stopped. The green spaces and the grass and trees, coming into full leaf as the days lengthened, were soothing and she felt herself relax as the sun warmed her. The weather, at least, was kind.

For the past few days, a young woman with blond hair had walked past, holding a small girl by the hand and pushing a pram. They had smiled at one another, although it seemed to take some effort from the young woman. On this particular morning it was too much of an effort, and tears filled her eyes.

'Why don't you come and sit down, at the end of the seat?' said Simone.

The woman, still holding the child's hand, sat down.

'Are you all right? You seem a bit upset.'

The woman started to cry.

'Don't cry, Mum, you'll wake the baby.'

She smiled through her tears.

'You're a good girl, Holly. Don't worry, I'm just a bit tired today.'

'It's a very strange time,' said Simone. 'We haven't had this sort of thing before. How are you managing?'

'It's pretty hard at the moment. My husband is working from home. He normally spends a lot of his time travelling, so he's a bit out of his element. It's hard for him to work with the children around, although Holly is very quiet and just gets on with things. But the baby is teething, so he cries quite a bit and Richard can't stand it.'

Simone nodded.

'Let's hope it doesn't go on for too long.'

'It's the atmosphere at home. It's a bit strained, to say the least.' She sighed. 'My name is Emily, by the way.'

'I'm Simone. I come here for a walk every day. I bring a coffee and a book. Perhaps we could meet again tomorrow. I'll bring two flasks, so we can have a socially distanced coffee morning together.'

'That would be lovely,' said Emily and stood up to leave.

The next morning, Simone prepared two flasks of coffee.

'I don't think you should be drinking so much coffee, Simone,' said Jean Paul.

'It's for my new friend Emily. We meet on Primrose Hill. She's beautiful and we enjoy talking.'

Over the next warm calm days, the highlight for Simone was her chats with Emily. She never knew how the young woman would be. Some days, she was bright and chatty. On others she looked pale and anxious. Simone found her vulnerability brought out protective feelings she didn't know she had.

Their conversations ranged from the simple description of the new words made by the baby to the discussion about the difficulties of being a wife and mother, especially during lockdown, when the usual norms of behaviour were being put under stress. When she discussed these chats with Jean Paul, he pointed out that Emily exemplified some of the challenges explored by Simone in her writings.

One morning, Emily didn't turn up. Simone sat drinking her own flask of coffee until well beyond the time of her usual arrival. When it started to rain, she left and walked home, accompanied by a feeling of anxiety.

'Why don't you text or phone her and ask how she is?' asked Jean Paul.

'I don't have her number, only just her first name.'

'So there's nothing you can do. I expect she'll be there tomorrow.'

Simone didn't sleep well that night. The next morning, she prepared two flasks of coffee.

'It's going to rain, Simone; she won't bring the children out in the rain. Stay home today.'

'No, I like the rain, and I just feel the need to go.'

When she arrived at their usual meeting place, Emily was already sitting on the seat with Holly, huddled under a big umbrella. The baby was sleeping in his pram. It was a grey day and London was invisible, shrouded in mist. It created an intimate atmosphere. Simone felt that it was just them in the whole of London. It was like a dream she had one night, when she took Emily into her arms. When she got closer, she had an intake of breath. Emily had bruises under her left eye and a cut at the edge of her mouth. She looked up as Simone approached but said nothing.

Simone sat down at the other end of the wet bench. She had no umbrella and just accepted being rained on.

'You look as if you could do with a coffee,' she said as she passed the flask to Emily.

Emily's hand shook as she poured the coffee into the beaker.

'He couldn't help it,' she whispered. 'The baby kept us awake all night and he had a deadline to meet. He just lost it.'

Simone stayed silent, looking at Emily. She very much wanted to hug her.

'He's like a pressure cooker, waiting to explode. He misses his work friends, there's no one to calm him down when the work gets tough. He always has been a bit controlling. That's why I don't have any friends, not that I could see them anyway right now.'

'Is Holly all right?' said Simone.

'He doesn't touch her. But she cries a lot, or else she's quiet and withdrawn.'

'Do you think it's safe to stay with him?'

'Well, I've nowhere else to go. I haven't told my parents. They've got enough on their plate. They're not in the best of health, so we can't go there because of the coronavirus.'

Simone felt helpless, not a feeling she was familiar or comfortable with.

'We can't do much at the moment,' she said. 'Let me think about it. Let's meet again tomorrow.'

By now, her hair was wet, and rain was running down her face. It looked and felt like tears. She stood up and smiled at Emily.

'I'll see you tomorrow, Emily.'

She didn't allow herself to look back as she walked away.

*

'You look bedraggled Simone; you'd better dry your hair. Why didn't you come home sooner?'

'I couldn't leave Emily. She's being abused by her husband. She has cuts and bruises.'

'That's terrible. What's she going to do? Leave him?'

'No. She has nowhere to go.'

'So she's just going with the flow?'

Simone didn't reply. All her instincts were telling her that Emily did have a choice; this belief was fundamental to her philosophy of life. She believed that people are what they make themselves to be. Yet she had a glimpse of the challenges facing her. If she acknowledged that freedom, it would be accompanied by anguish. She had the freedom to leave, but with the anguish of facing an unknown, perhaps difficult future. Emily had to consider not just her own position but the future of her children.

'I'd like to help her, Jean Paul. What can we do?'

'We can't do anything until she takes some responsibility herself. You know that.'

'Yes of course. But I want to at least offer her a chance.'

'Be careful, Simone. It's her life. If she leaves her husband, she'll be the one who has to live with the repercussions, not you.'

Simone spent the rest of the day reading parts of her updated book. A lot of it was exploring the oppression of women. In her next version of it, if she ever got to that stage, she would include a section on the effect of a lockdown. Perhaps she would write an essay about it now. She struggled to fit some of her ideas into the current reality of social distancing and staying home messaging from the government. The evening was uncomfortable, not even soothed by glasses of wine.

'Do you think I've got it all wrong?' she said.

'What do you mean?'

'It's fine theorising about searching for identity and meaning. In practice, having children and an abusing husband throws a spanner in the works.'

'It definitely doesn't help,' said Jean Paul.

*

After a disturbed night, when she tossed and turned unable to relax into sleep, Simone declined breakfast and prepared her two flasks of coffee. The weather had taken a turn for the better and promised a warm and sunny morning. Primrose Hill appeared welcoming, blossom on trees, birds singing, blue sky, the external world that brings pleasure and delight.

In contrast Simone's internal world was grey. She sat on her usual bench to wait for Emily and the children.

When they appeared, they looked like a happy young family. As they approached, she could hear Emily singing along with her young daughter while the baby sat wide awake in his pram seeming to enjoy his surroundings. Simone wondered if she had imagined the previous day's problems, but she hadn't, because the bruises, although faded, could still be seen despite Emily's attempts to cover them with makeup.

'It's a lovely day, Simone, I'm really looking forward to the coffee you bring. It's how I like it. It's like French coffee.'

'That's what it is,' said Simone. 'I always bring some with me when I travel. It helps me to remember who I am. Everything all right with you?'

'Richard was charming yesterday. His work went well, he even cooked supper. It was just the lockdown that made him lose his temper. He's fine now.'

Simone smiled and poured herself a coffee.

'That's good. If you yearn to get away, I am looking for a research assistant. You could come with me to France. I'm planning to return as soon as this lockdown is over.'

'It's tempting, Simone, thank you. But I couldn't go to France, my parents are here and old and vulnerable and I couldn't leave Richard, he needs me.'

Simone sighed and said nothing.

'What are you doing for yourself during the lockdown, Emily?'

'Lots of reading, but I'm running out of books.'

'I can lend you some. I'll bring a couple tomorrow.'

*

The days passed and most mornings Emily and Simone sat on the seat on Primrose Hill, looked over London and drank strong French coffee. The weather became sunny and warm, day after day and they tentatively learned more about each other. Emily, who had qualified as an accountant, had been looking for some freelance work before the lockdown. On some days, she was quiet and withdrawn. Although she said nothing, Simone knew that she was still being abused in some way.

'Do you think we could exchange phone numbers?' asked Simone.

Emily looked startled.

'Well, let me give you mine, and feel free to call or text me.'

At last, the lockdown came to an end. It was still summer, and Simone and Jean Paul had rented a cottage on the north Devon coast. They planned to walk by the sea, and on Exmoor. The cottage had three bedrooms, so they invited Emily and the children to join them for a few days. Richard stayed at home; he had more deadlines to meet. Jean Paul was looking forward to meeting Emily and the children. They spent the days on the beach and Simone could see both Emily and Holly relaxing as they spent long afternoons playing in the sand and running into the sea. Simone and Jean Paul looked after the baby.

'You would have made a splendid mother,' he told her as she fed the baby and cuddled him to sleep.

'Only for a few days,' she said.

The evenings were spent in the cottage garden, Holly

running around until her bedtime. When both children were asleep the three of them sat together drinking wine and talking about the day.

'It's been lovely to be with you. I feel so safe. I've started to read the books you lent me, Simone. I suppose that I've not thought about things until now. Women do seem to be the second sex; now you've pointed it out, it's obvious. There's a lot of pressure to just go with the flow. It's the easy way.'

'It is harder for women than men,' said Jean Paul, 'to live an authentic life.'

'I don't even know what that means. I just do what my mother did and all the women I know do the same.'

'Do you think they're happy?' said Simone.

'No. I can see that some of my friends are being reduced, even crushed, by their marriages. They believed it was their destiny, but after a while some of them feel their lives are being wasted.'

'How do you feel?' asked Jean Paul. 'Only answer if you wish,' he added.

'It's OK, I love my children and I love Richard, most of the time. But sometimes I think, is this it? Then I tell myself I'm being ungrateful and selfish.'

'That's part of the way we are controlled,' said Simone. 'It takes away our freedom.'

'It's interesting to hear your ideas,' said Emily. 'It's been a busy day, so I think I'll go up to bed now, I have a long drive tomorrow.'

Simone and Jean Paul enjoyed the rest of their stay in the cottage. They took long walks on Exmoor during the balmy sunny days, spent quiet reading times and peaceful evenings with a few drinks and then dinner. They didn't discuss Emily although she was often in Simone's thoughts.

When they returned to London, Simone wanted to restart her morning walks and coffee with Emily. But she had so much to do for the first few days that she didn't have time. After a few days she prepared the two flasks of French coffee and walked to the seat on Primrose Hill. Although she waited for an hour, there was no sign of Emily. When she got back to the flat, she explained that she felt concerned.

'You haven't been for a few days either, perhaps she thinks you are still away. She'll probably be there tomorrow.'

But she wasn't. Nor did she appear for the rest of the week.

Simone tried to get on with her work. The new essay occupied much of her attention. Every morning she went to the seat with the two flasks of French coffee. She saw other people to chat to but there was no sign of Emily and her children.

'I think it's time we returned to Paris,' said Jean Paul. 'If the conference is rearranged it will be a virtual one, so we can be anywhere. I'm missing our friends. I've had enough of London, and I'd like to go home before anything else happens.'

So they made the arrangements and booked their flight home.

The flight was in the evening and on their last morning, Simone walked to the seat on Primrose Hill. There was someone sitting on the seat and her spirits lifted. When she got closer, she could see it wasn't Emily.

*

Back in their flat in Paris, they settled back into their usual routines. Things were not back to normal, but they were able to meet some friends and go out to cafés. Simone longed for Emily and hoped that she was safe. Since she couldn't contact her, she had to make do with memories and fantasies.

Then one evening, Simone's mobile rang.

'Simone, it's Emily.'

'It's really good to hear from you, Emily. How are you? I've missed our morning coffee meetings.'

'Something awful has happened.'

Simone just listened. Emily spoke fast and sounded strange.

'Richard's been angry and aggressive all day. I put the children to bed early. He came upstairs and started shouting, shoving me against the wall and hitting me.'

She sobbed and went on, 'So I fought him off for once, and pushed him. He fell down the stairs. He's either dead or unconscious. I don't know what to do.'

'Call an ambulance. It's not your fault. Ring me again when you've done that, OK?'

Simone waited. She walked up and down their small kitchen and looked out of the window at the warm summer evening. Her phone rang and she picked it up with a shaking hand.

'It's Emily. I think he's dead, there's no point in calling an ambulance. I just need to get away. Will you help me?'

'Are you sure he's dead?'

'I think so. But I can't stay here with him any longer. He frightens me. I've been thinking about what you said. It's bad for the children, he's abusing them too. I'm going to leave. Will you help me?'

Simone paused, for what seemed to her a long time, but was only a few seconds.

'Yes Emily. There is a late train to Paris. Take the children and go to the station. If you can't get on the train, stay there until the first train the next morning. When you know which train you are on, text me. I'll meet you at the Gare du Nord.'

'Thank you, Simone.'

Simone sank down onto a kitchen stool, thinking about what she had agreed to do. Her heart was racing. She reminded herself that she believed that a person could only exercise their freedom when it is accepted and supported by others around them. So she must support Emily. She was also taken by the thought that Emily would be with her, here in Paris. She smiled at that prospect. Jean Paul was in his study working on an essay. She told him what she had agreed with Emily.

'Is this a good idea, Simone?'

'I want to have her here with me. I want to help her.'

'As you wish,' he said and returned to his writing. She would go by herself to the station.

After two hours, a long wait for Simone, she received a text from Emily.

'Arriving at a quarter to twelve with the children.'

*

The train journey seemed to last forever. Eventually, the children slept, and Emily allowed herself to think about Richard. He had always bullied her, and the children had made his behaviour worse. She was running away and felt relief through her exhaustion.

At the station, with the baby in a pushchair and dragging along a sleepy Holly, Emily ran towards Simone. Simone held her close in a hug, as she sobbed into her shoulder. Holly looked up and gave Simone a weak smile.

'I'll get us a taxi to the apartment. Holly is more than ready for bed. Then we'll have a chat.'

With Holly and the baby asleep in the guest bedroom, Jean Paul poured both women a glass of brandy.

'What's the situation, Emily?' he asked. His voice was kind but stern.

'If I could just stay here for a while. I can't face being back in London. Richard is probably dead. I really don't know what to do.'

'Of course you can,' said Simone. 'You can help me with my research, and I would welcome your opinion on my writing.'

Jean Paul said nothing.

The next two days were an education for Emily as she wandered about Paris, pushing the baby in the pram. She pushed thoughts of Richard to the back of her mind. Holly and Simone formed a close bond, holding hands as Simone regularly bent down to show and explain something interesting to the little girl. Emily's greatest education was helping Simone with her work during a wet afternoon, discussing her ideas and surprising herself with her own understanding and contributions.

That evening Emily received a call on her mobile. Simone was watching when she answered it and saw her face blanch. She looked as if she might faint. She listened to her responses.

'Yes Richard, the children are fine. I'm sorry to have worried my parents, I'll phone and tell them that we are all fine. I'm staying with a friend. I can't cope with it at home right now. I'll let you know how things go.' Then she ended the call.

'Good for you,' said Simone. 'That was brave.'

Emily was still shaking.

'He's not dead then,' said Jean Paul.

'No, he was just unconscious. He thinks he fell down the stairs because he had too much to drink.'

*

To Simone, the summer, which left Paris empty of her friends and colleagues, was usually a time to travel to the sea. This year, she relished the quiet streets where she could wander with her new friend without questions being asked or comments made. They sometimes held hands while Simone explained some historical landmark, but Emily would remove her hand if other people were around. Although Jean Paul and Simone accepted each other's right to take a lover, Emily and Simone did not make the final step to physical intimacy.

Time passed and people began to return to Paris. Jean Paul began to go out alone in the evenings to meet friends.

'When are you going to get back to a normal life, Simone? You're missing out, there are some new philosophies being discussed. People are wondering what's happened to you.'

By early September, Simone's friends had returned. She felt mixed emotions about introducing Emily to them. She intended to keep the two parts of her life as separate as possible. It put a distance between her and Jean Paul. Some nights the baby couldn't settle and cried for what seemed like hours to Simone and there were moments when she yearned for her previous life. Nevertheless, she determined to uphold her personal values and support Emily, who she loved but also pitied.

Gradually she started to feel the constraints of the circumstances she had willingly put herself into. However, Emily was getting well into reading and in other ways helping Simone with research. Without the fear of abuse, she was learning to create herself, encouraged by both Simone and eventually Jean Paul. She blossomed and looked even more beautiful, and Holly became an inquisitive child who laughed a lot. They all knew it couldn't last, but no one wanted to be the person who caused the bold experiment to come to an end. Emily and Simone spent hours together every day. As they grew closer, Jean Paul observed and worked hard to remain loving to Simone and celebrate her freedom to love Emily.

It was Holly who first began to disturb the equilibrium.

'Mum, when can we go home? I want to go to school and see my friends.'

Simone realised that in their mutual delight, Emily and she had neglected to think about Holly.

It was the beginning of the end. From that moment, they all knew that Emily would soon leave with the children. Simone had written about freedom being accompanied by anguish. When she took Emily and the children to the station, it took all her strength to smile and kiss and hug Holly and Emily and talk about planning to get together again soon.

She couldn't stay to see the train leave the station. It would have been too difficult, too painful.

When she got back to the apartment, Jean Paul was in his study. He came out to greet her and held out his arms. She was grateful for his bearlike hug.

'Don't waste it, Simone,' he said. 'Write about it.'

The Crossing

The truck moved slowly down the metal ramp into the bowels of the ferry. George parked it, as instructed by a crew member, tight against the wall of the ship. Then he picked up his bag and clambered out of his cab down onto the deck. The noise was deafening as lorries, caravans and cars drove into position, as close as possible to each other. He didn't linger but walked to the exit door and walked up five flights of stairs to find his cabin. It had been a long drive, over several days, from the south of Spain to the Port of Bilbao. The twenty-four-hour crossing would give him the opportunity for a bit of a rest, as well as the chance to explore his other interest.

He had a routine, developed over a decade of long-distance driving. He looked too slight of build to be driving such a huge truck. But power steering meant that physical strength wasn't too much of an issue and despite his slender frame, he was wiry and strong. His first activity after depositing his overnight bag in his cabin was to go to the lounge where the truckers usually hung out. It was at the back of the ferry, with a huge semicircular window from where there was a panoramic view, a semicircular bar and round tables lit from beneath, with glass tops that looked like a compass. He ordered a drink and sipped the cold tonic water as he watched the ship slowly pull away from the dock.

His hand shook a little as the usual excitement began to grow. Other truckers started to fill the lounge. One or two he had met on previous crossings, so they sat together and made desultory conversation about their trip and where they were headed when they got to the UK.

After about an hour, pleading the need to have a bit of a rest, he left them and started his reconnoitre of the ship and passengers. First he went to the passenger café, got himself a coffee and sat down to look around. He enjoyed observing a handsome young man, by himself, sitting reading a book. He was totally engrossed and underlined passages as he read. *He's delightful but too young*, George concluded, and stood up to continue his observations in another part of the ship. He had better luck in the shop, where he noticed an older man buying a toothbrush and other toiletries and an adapter for electrical appliances. He bought an English newspaper, so he clearly could speak English. George bought himself a bottle of red wine, French and rather expensive. He left the shop with his purchase and went to his cabin. A few hours' sleep was what he needed.

Part of his routine was to have an early dinner in the Drivers' Lounge which was open between 6 and 8.30 pm. It was a pleasant area of the ship, separated from the main passenger restaurant by a corridor with a five-foot-high wall of opaque glass. He could just about see into the restaurant as he walked to the Drivers' Lounge. There was no sign of the man he had spotted in the shop. He sat at a Formica-topped table to eat his dinner. A few of the other drivers joined him. Gradually the passenger restaurant began to fill up; the noise level of conversation and wine bottles being opened and poured increased.

'I don't think I'll be joining you in the bar tonight,' he said to his fellow drivers. 'I need to get my head down. Got a long drive from Portsmouth up to Scotland. Another couple of days on the road.'

They nodded and returned to their food and chat. As he left the lounge and walked through the corridor between the restaurants, he saw the man from the shop, dining alone. A smile tickled the corner of his mouth, as he anticipated the excitement to come.

Back in his cabin, he unpacked his bag and laid out his clothes on the bunk. He undressed and stepped into the small shower. *Let the transformation begin.*

In the shower, he shaved his legs and washed his hair. He had never had much facial hair. What he did have, he removed with cream, so as to avoid the growth of stubble. After towelling himself dry, he started to dress, allowing himself to enjoy the feel of the silky underwear. This evening's outfit was a long-sleeved royal blue silk blouse and a calf-length straight black leather skirt. He had learned, over time, not to overdo it. Elegant rather than sexy, and not too striking and flamboyant. He didn't want too many people to notice him. As he put on the sensual clothes, he felt himself slip into role. The wig completed the transformation, dark brown, mid-length, with a fringe. With the antique silver drop earrings, he thought he looked rather European and interesting. The only part of his transformation that he found difficult was the shoes. High heels were just too ridiculous and hurt his feet. The compromise was a pair of expensive black soft leather shoes with kitten heels. Being petite was part of the transformation, so they worked well enough. He applied a discreet amount of makeup, mainly emphasising his blue eyes and finished the preparations with a spray of perfume.

His capacious leather handbag looked as if had cost a fortune, but it had no identifying logos and could have come from any number of designers. Into it he put the bottle of red wine, a corkscrew, a book, and some tablets, known as date rape drugs, which were vital to the success of the operation, as well as a leather purse containing cash, no credit cards, a comb, and a powder compact. All his personal possessions, including his mobile phone, he packed away and put the bag under the bunk. He checked his watch, not the one he usually wore when driving, but a delicate gold bracelet watch which he had bought from a second-hand jewellery shop in London. It was nearly nine o'clock. Dinner would have finished by now for the man dining alone. He listened at the door of his cabin and, when all seemed quiet, he let himself out and made his way to the bar.

The large bar at the back of the ferry was crowded. A few fellow drivers were well into their drinking evening and didn't even look up when he passed. A good sign. The man he had chosen for the evening wasn't in the bar. A chill of disappointment ran through him. The bar was on two levels, so he went up the metal spiral staircase to the next level. Relief and a flicker of excitement as his adrenalin started to flow. He was sitting, alone, at a small table tucked in the corner. The bar was busy, with no empty tables so it seemed acceptable to enquire, 'Would you mind if I sat at your table?'

'Please do.' He indicated the chair opposite him. A waiter came over to take an order for drinks.

'I'll have a glass of red wine,' to the waiter. 'Thank you. I'm Georgina, by the way.'

'Good evening. I'm Richard. Pleased to meet you.'

George could see that he had made a good choice. From the Rolex wristwatch to the pale pink cashmere sweater, and the hand-made brown loafer shoes, Richard was obviously not short of money. The waiter brought the red wine and Richard ordered a glass for himself. They engaged in small talk for a while, discussing the weather and the thankfully calm crossing. Gradually Georgina turned up the charm, smiling and encouraging him to talk about himself. It wasn't difficult. He seemed to come out of his shell as the wine began to have an effect. Georgina moved her chair closer and could sense his interest increasing. He explained that he was a salesman, of rare books. He had been to Barcelona to look at some unusual books about Anton Gaudi.

'Did you know that he had a thing about dragons?' he said.

'How fascinating. Did you find anything?'

'Yes, a book of his preliminary drawings for some of his art installations. I'm taking it to London to see if I can get it properly verified as his work. There are plenty of fakes about, so I need to check it out.'

'I'd love to see it, Richard. Do you have it with you?'

'It's locked away in my cabin. It could be quite valuable. But I could show you if you like.'

'It's getting a bit noisy here anyway. That would be good. I bought a bottle of wine in the shop earlier on today, so it seems like a perfect way to end the evening.'

They got up and Richard led the way to his cabin. It was a grade up from the one George occupied. They sat on the bunks opposite to one another. There were two glasses in the shower room and Georgina offered to rinse them and open the bottle of wine. She poured two large glasses and while Richard was retrieving the book from the suitcase in the wardrobe, she slipped a tablet into his glass of wine.

'Cheers! Let's hope the book is the genuine article,' said Richard.

'How much would it be worth, then?'

'Could be a six-figure sum.'

'Wow. That's awesome. Do you think it's genuine?'

'Yes, I do. I've already been in touch with a few of my contacts about it. There seems to be a lot of interest.'

George watched as the drug began to take effect. Richard's eyes started to close, and he slumped back onto his bunk. He had judged the dose, amplified by the alcohol, to cause amnesia and sleepiness but no worse. He knew that the effect would last for about six hours, by which time Georgina would have changed back to George, a trucker, with no link to the attractive woman who had supposedly seduced Richard. When he was sure that Richard was well out of it, he removed his Rolex watch, and searched his wallet for cash. He was happy with pounds or euros but took no credit or debit cards. They were too risky, and he wasn't looking for any more than small pickings, just to supplement his trucker's pay. On a whim he took the book of supposedly Gaudi sketches. They were charming, and for some reason he wanted to own them. He listened at the cabin door, and when he felt sure there was no-one around, he quietly slipped away and returned to his own quarters. He sat on his bunk and poured himself a glass of wine. As he enjoyed the taste, he savoured being in his sensual clothes. The watch and book were packed away in his bag. *A good evening*, he thought.

The next morning, when advised over the ship loudspeaker, with the other drivers he went down to rejoin his huge truck. As he navigated the customs checks, he smiled to himself. He had a drive from Portsmouth, but it was to Kent, not Scotland. He was looking forward to a few days off, spent with his wife and children, before his next assignment.

Richard woke up with a bad headache. He couldn't remember what had happened the previous evening, which he took to mean that he had done something silly. Eventually he became aware that something was wrong. He couldn't locate the book of Gaudi drawings. After searching every inch of his cabin, he came to the conclusion that it had been stolen, but he had no idea by whom or how it had happened. He slowly remembered that he had invited a woman back to his cabin and blushed with embarrassment. Perhaps it was as well that he couldn't remember the details. He thought of reporting it to the ship security people. Then he thought better of it. He couldn't afford for his partner to find out how disloyal he had been. He put aside, for the time being, the problem of explaining the absence of the Gaudi drawings.

*

Over the next couple of months, George made several crossings on the ferry between Bilbao and Portsmouth. Usually there was someone travelling alone who provided an opportunity for a little drug-assisted robbery. He knew that he was running the risk of being caught, but the adventure gave him such a lot of pleasure and excitement that he kept taking the risk. He had a scare on one occasion when one of the waiters passed a comment, 'Good evening, madam, your usual red wine?'

He reluctantly made the decision to take a break from the activity. The book he had taken from Richard was safely locked away at home, since he couldn't decide what to do with it. The twenty-four-hour ferry journey seemed tedious without the pleasure of wearing sensual clothes and an evening spiced with risk.

Richard had thought long and hard about whether to report the missing, presumably stolen, watch and book. He wasn't too bothered about the Rolex watch, a bit too flashy for his taste, but he mourned the loss of the Gaudi drawings. However, his shame and embarrassment prevented him from taking any action.

*

After what he considered to be a long enough break, George made the decision to resume his pleasures. As a precaution, he bought a new wig and some clothes that were very different from his previous choice. He decided to go blond, with a short and spiky haircut, and dress in black leggings and a loose purple shirt. The finishing touch was a pair of wire-framed glasses. He wasn't altogether sure the outfit would be as effective as before, but he couldn't risk someone noticing the same woman on a regular basis. He liked the outfit himself; it was youthful and fun.

As per his usual routine, after depositing his bag in his cabin, he went to the bar to have a drink with the other drivers. He walked into the bar, and there he was, sitting alone at the same table in the corner. It was Richard, he was sure, but he looked about ten years older. His complexion looked almost grey, and he had an air of despondency hanging around him, like a cloud. Seeing him almost stopped George in his tracks. He felt bad to see Richard a shadow of his former self.

In a decision that surprised him, he walked over to his table.

'Do you mind if I join you?' he asked.

Richard looked up. 'Help yourself,' he said.

When the waiter came to take his order, George ordered a beer. 'Can I get you something?' he asked Richard.

'Thank you. A gin and tonic would be good.'

They both looked out of the window at the receding port of Bilbao. When their drinks arrived, George held up his glass.

'Good health,' he said.

Richard gave the ghost of a smile. 'To better times.'

George nodded. 'Life's full of ups and downs.'

'Seems to be more down than up at the moment,' said Richard sadly. 'I've had a bit of bad luck lately. It's taking me a while to get back on my feet.'

George drank a few large gulps of beer and looked as if he was prepared to listen.

'Lost my reputation, that's the problem,' said Richard. 'Nobody believes my word any longer.'

'What caused that?'

'I found a very special book, by Gaudi, I picked it up in Barcelona. That's my trade. A beautiful book, worth a fortune. But it was stolen. Unfortunately, I'd already told a dealer about it and he even had some clients lined up to buy it, so he was furious when I couldn't produce it. He even suggested that I had invented the whole story. We haven't spoken since, but these things get out and nobody wants to do business with me now. Spent years building my business and more importantly, my reputation. It's trashed now.'

George put his beer down. He didn't feel like drinking any more. He looked at the wreck of the man in front of him and felt uncomfortable. Thoughts were rushing about in his head. This was all his fault. Stealing from well-off people was one thing, destroying another human being was completely different.

'I don't know what to say. Sounds like real tough luck.'

They sat in silence, looking out at the gradually darkening sky.

'I need to go and have a rest,' said George. 'Got a busy day tomorrow.'

When he returned to his cabin, George sat on his bunk to think. At his usual time, he joined the other truckers for dinner in the Drivers' Lounge. He didn't feel very hungry so didn't eat much. When he left, he saw that Richard was dining alone, picking at his food and looking the picture of misery. That was it; George made his decision.

Back in his cabin, his began his transformation. He became a blond fun-loving woman who was determined to cheer Richard up. He found him in the bar. He hadn't really worked out how to approach him, so sat at a table next to his and opened the book he had brought with him. In a while he noticed Richard looking at the book cover.

'It's a good read,' he said. 'Have you read it? It was shortlisted for the Booker Prize but didn't win.'

They started a conversation about books they had read and enjoyed. After a while they exchanged names. George was now Becky. He thought the name went with his new persona. An hour and a few drinks later Richard certainly seemed more cheerful. He had explained about his book collecting and that he had a bookshop which sold second-hand books. It was in London on the Charing Cross Road. Becky had no intention of going back to Richard's cabin. He didn't want to rob him, he just wanted to help him feel better and it looked as if he had succeeded.

'Well, Richard, thank you for a very pleasant evening. You've made my trip. I wish you and your bookshop well.'

'It's been a pleasure to spend the evening with you, Becky.'

*

A week later, Richard got to his bookshop in time to open up and receive the morning deliveries. As usual there were parcels of books. He opened them with pleasure, as usual. There was one rather badly wrapped parcel that he left until last. It contained the book of Gaudi drawings.

The Truth Trap

It happened during the coronavirus lockdown. Whether that caused it, is a moot point.

I often leave my car on the street outside my house. I have a garage, but it's just too much of a fag putting a big car in a small garage, so I don't. There's so little traffic that it seemed pointless. I only use it to do my shopping because you can't go anywhere else. To cut to the chase, I'm in such a funny state, due to all this stuff that's going on, that I left my mobile phone in the car and the next day it wasn't there. I hadn't even bothered to lock the car. My focus is a bit sloppy these weird days. Not a big problem, you might think, because it was old and a "pay as you go" phone. Apparently, so I've been told, they are quite popular with petty criminals. Being phone-free during lockdown, however, seemed like one of my worst nightmares. It provided my only contact with my family and friends, apart from a few neighbours, who come singly and sit in my garden for a cup of tea and home-made cake. They have made life so much better; I don't know how I would have managed without them during this time of isolation.

I told Patrick, one of my neighbours, as I poured him a second cup, what had happened.

'No problem, love, I bought Janet a new phone for her

birthday and haven't got rid of the old one. You can have that until you can get a new one.'

'Will she mind you giving me the phone?'

'Not at all. She's delighted with the new one, she always doing FaceTime with the grandchildren. She says she can't imagine life without it now, so you're very welcome to have the old one. I'll drop it in on my way to the allotment.'

I'm a bit slow with tech stuff, but Patrick is a computer nerd, so he had done what was necessary and had even charged the phone, so it was ready to go. First I contacted my friends and family to inform them of my new number. A few of them texted a reply, so I wasn't surprised when early one morning, while I was still in bed, I heard the ping of an arriving message. I have never had a text like it. It was the sexiest few short lines I have ever read. There was no sign-off and I didn't recognise the number of the sender. I have to say that it was rather an uplifting start to the day. Who sent it? In my mind I ran down a list of possibilities. None of them seemed at all likely, but you never know what lurks underneath a proper persona. Some of these austere academics I work with might be brimming over with passion, however unlikely it seems. I decided to wait on further developments.

The next morning, nothing. I saw Patrick on his early morning jog and decided not to bother getting out of bed to wave. The following morning as I was drinking my tea, in bed, just after Patrick had jogged past, the ping indicated another early text. It was blush-making.

It was a poem:

SEX: A PARADOX
Is it
A blessing or a curse,
A giving or a taking,
Power or submission.
Liberation or imprisonment.

An answer to a question,
A benefit or a liability,
An opening or a closing,
A truth or a lie.

Possession or letting go,
Forever or the moment,
The end of the beginning or
The beginning of the end.

Do I
Give in strength or weakness,
Moan for pleasure or pain,
Weep for joy or sorrow.
Does it matter?

The texts arrived every morning, each one sexy enough to increase my pulse rate. On the fifth morning it said, 'See you, same time, and same place. Can't wait.'

I felt my spirits drop. So these sexy texts weren't for me after all. Amid the anxiety and gloom of lockdown, they had been fun and exciting. Almost a reason for getting up in the morning. Then it hit me. It wasn't really my phone; the texts had been meant for the proper owner, Patrick's wife, Janet. As this gradually dawned on me, I saw Patrick returning from his run; so they were sent while he was out jogging. I had been friends with Patrick, and particularly with his wife, Janet, for years. I thought we were close friends, but obviously not that close, since she hadn't told me about this. I knew that she and Patrick had been irritated with each other lately, but I put it down to being together all the time. I wondered about this sexy lover and whether Patrick had any idea.

It's pretty boring being in lockdown when you live alone. Well, that's my excuse for what I did. I replied to the text message.

My text said:

'How about meeting somewhere else, since the weather is so lovely? I'll meet you on the towpath by the town bridge at 7 pm.'

Without giving myself the chance to think it through and change my mind, I sent it, with a whoosh. It certainly bucked up the day. I had something to think about and plan. I wouldn't be breaking any lockdown rules because I regularly took my daily exercise along the towpath. Usually, I wouldn't be bothered about how I looked, but now I had a reason to consider my dress. It made an energising change after the weeks of anxiety and apathy.

As seven o'clock approached, I nearly changed my mind, but I had just finished reading an interesting book and needed something new to stimulate my little grey cells. Janet, the woman he would be expecting to meet, had a colourful and slightly whacky dress style. I decided to stick to my own style, which is more elegant, or so I've been told. I had spent an entertaining afternoon deciding how I would deal with the meeting. If he looked interesting, I would find a way of loitering and striking up a conversation when the person he was planning to meet didn't arrive. It crossed my mind that it could be a woman, but when I re-read the texts that seemed highly unlikely.

I arrived at the bridge a few minutes before seven. There was no-one there, so I walked on past along the towpath for a few minutes and sat down on a conveniently placed seat. It had red tape across it to discourage people sitting on it, so I just pushed it to the back of the seat and perched on the front, which was most uncomfortable. After a long five minutes, I saw a man arrive. Shock, horror, it was Patrick.

I stayed frozen in position and looked down at my smart shoes while I tried to figure out what to do. From the corner of my eye, I saw him approach the seat.

'Hello Jackie, shall we walk back, socially distanced of course?'

I felt my face burn with embarrassment, but I stood up and gave him what I hoped was a challenging glare.

'What's going on, Patrick? Did you send those texts?'

'Yes, I did. I surprised even myself.'

'Did you intend them for me, or for Janet?'

'That's a truth trap, Jackie.'

'What do you mean?'

'Well, you may not like the answer when I tell you the truth.'

We walked along in silence for a while. The evening was beautiful, warm with a gentle breeze rippling the water on the river, which was home to a record amount of bird life. The lockdown had had a few positive effects.

'I thought I was sending them to my wife. Things have been bad between us now for some time. Being in lockdown together with nothing to dilute the tedium has not been helpful, to put it mildly, so I thought I would try to liven things up a bit. I forgot that I had given her phone to you. As soon as the first one was sent, I realised my mistake. After the initial panic, it felt like an opportunity. So when I sent the next ones, they were meant for you.'

My confusion must have shown on my face.

'You know that I've been interested in you, and I can tell you are in me.'

I didn't contradict him.

'Being in lockdown has shown me how much I need excitement and new experiences,' I said. 'Hence my response to your text messages. But I didn't know who they were from, so that mystery was part of it.'

'So now you know they were from me?' he asked quietly.

'We're back in the truth trap. Right now, I don't know how I feel about it. We could be just two bored people trying to survive lockdown.'

'I suppose you're right. Or it could have given us the time to think about how we want our future to be, if there is one, after this.'

I didn't reply because I wasn't sure how to. For the first time I was glad these weird times ruled out close physical contact. We continued to walk slowly home without speaking.

When we got to my house, I made a shocking decision.

'Would you like to come in for a drink, Patrick? In the garden?'

He nodded and followed me into my house and out into the darkening evening. We sat quietly drinking our wine; his phone pinged. He looked at the message.

'It's Janet, I have to go. Sorry.'

I sat alone until it started to get chilly. I thought about the poem he had sent and decided that if I had the chance, I would explore the paradox.

Over the next week I only saw Patrick at a distance when the neighbours came out into their separate gardens to say hello over a coffee. My pulse rate increased when I remembered his text messages. He had suggested, via text, that we meet as if by chance, while taking our daily exercise. I agreed to meet him two days later. After I had made the decision, I couldn't settle to my usual routine and reading a book was impossible, I felt too restless. I must have been in a bit of a state, I can't think how else it could have happened. I'm usually so organised. The phone rang, and in my rush to answer it, I tripped, fell, and hit my head on the sofa. When I tried to get up, I couldn't put my weight on the right foot. Over the next couple of hours, I saw my ankle swell. I had taken my shoe off and it was obvious that I wouldn't be able to wear it for a few days. When I had slightly recovered from the shock, I phoned my next-door neighbour. She came at once, suggested that I needed to put my foot up and rest, and volunteered to do my shopping until I was mobile again.

My daily exercise was out of the question, so meeting Patrick as we had planned was abandoned. I sent him a text to explain and as it whooshed I felt a whiff of relief. I wouldn't have to resolve the paradox of sex with him. It could remain a paradox for the foreseeable future, and I could continue to be able to look my neighbours and my friend Janet in the eye.

Never Say Die

She was definitely feeling scared; in fear of her life, even. She knew she had enemies, plenty of them. She daren't even go to some countries because she was hated, not by everyone, but by those who had the power. So she stayed well clear, for the time being, anyway. She thought she was safe in Europe, where she had friends and supporters.

However, lately she had begun to sense a change for the worse, even in Europe, and in her special place, the UK. Things were not looking good. Inequality was increasing, working people had stagnating wages and no job security. Some even had zero hours contracts. London was becoming a tax haven and a centre for money laundering, with housing that was too expensive for ordinary working people.

She knew she had enemies even here and they seemed to be getting stronger, so for the first time in decades she was feeling sick and frightened. When she mentioned this to her friends they said, 'Don't worry, Democracy, you'll be fine.'

She didn't feel particularly reassured. The fat cats, who did all they could to undermine her, were getting fatter. They thought she was a huge source of trouble and preferred Fred Capitalism who was making an excellent job of looking after them. He was on their side and helping and encouraging them to get richer and richer. He thought rising inequality was nothing to do with him and if it meant that there was more poverty, well what was that to him. 'Just the fall-out,' he said. 'Tough up and get on with it.'

Her friends often asked her, 'What are you all about, Democracy?'

'I am about government by the people; every eligible person should have a say,' she replied.

They also asked her about Fred Capitalism. One of them said, 'Fred Capitalism has created a useless class of parasitical rentiers.'

'Strong words,' said Democracy. 'What do you mean?'

'They just use their money to make more,' said her friend.

*

Fred Capitalism had some powerful friends. Well, not friends exactly, more old cronies. His best friend was Big Business. Some of them were owners of newspapers and controlled the media. They were quick to applaud the successes of Fred and were happy to distract their readers with stories of sex, scandals and sport, with a hefty sprinkling of royal tours and goings-on. So their readers were not even aware that Democracy was sad and frightened. She was not without friends in the media but not enough to make much of an impact.

She had lots of other friends, or at least she thought she did. Politicians were supposed to be her friends, but these days she was beginning to get a few whiffs of doubt about that. Some of them behaved as though they were a law unto themselves. They were pretty close with Big Business and seemed to be perfectly happy to do all they could to help them, even if it was at the expense of the country. They did nothing to stop big takeover bids and seemed keen to sell off every national organisation even when it was doing OK.

Sadly, Democracy could think of many changes that would not have occurred if she had been stronger. Like Big Business running the train service. She worried that it was the thin end of the wedge and that there was plenty more of that to come. Big Business was insatiable and since Fred Capitalism had gone global, he had access to money from all around the world and was pretty keen to buy things, especially power and influence.

Democracy knew that she wasn't perfect. She was still very young and inexperienced. She had plenty of faults. Winston Churchill had criticised her but then he said that when you look at the alternatives, she wasn't so bad. So she knew that she had a lot to live up to and it was becoming increasingly challenging.

It wasn't helped by the fact that Fred Capitalism was supported by whole departments of economists in universities and think tanks around the world, especially in the USA. They thought everything to do with money could be understood by equations. They were completely divorced from any other areas of study, such as sociology or ethics. They came up with theories such as the "trickledown effect" and based policies on it, even though they had no evidence to support it.

Big Business looked pretty sharp and trendy, very 21st century. They had slogans such as "Don't be evil", but in the view of some, they were just that, slogans.

Several events had happened in the last decade which showed Democracy she really was in danger. The effects of the banking crisis were still being felt, except by those people who had caused it in the first place. They were just carrying on getting richer with their huge salaries and bonuses. Democracy thought that some of them should be in jail.

Although she was young, Democracy was no fool. As she said to her friends, 'Fred Capitalism is getting stronger. He's global now and seems to be unstoppable.'

'So what about the regulators?' said her friends. 'Can't they keep him in check?'

'No, I'm afraid not, well at least they haven't managed to so far.'

'Don't despair,' they said. 'There is an election soon. Maybe that will restore some sort of balance. The people know that inequality is increasing. They will surely be concerned and vote for some changes.'

With every election, Democracy felt her spirits rise. The fact that there were elections made her happy, even although the process left a lot to be desired. It gave The People a chance to change things, at least in a small way. She knew that a change in government would have only a marginal effect on Fred Capitalism and Big Business, but you had to start somewhere.

Democracy knew that Fred Capitalism wasn't all bad. He had helped to raise people's standard of living even if there was vast inequality. He encouraged innovation and development, at least if there was money to be made. But he was getting bloated and rotten, and Democracy couldn't see how she could get rid of him or even whether that was the answer.

Yet from time to time, things happened that brought joy to her heart. Social media helped, especially in those countries where Democracy was frightened to go. There were blogs and tweets which reminded her that she was needed and wanted, so she mustn't give up. She needed a strategy to overcome her enemies and to strengthen her friends.

She knew that her greatest resource was The People. People who would understand how important she was, and how dangerous the world would be if she sickened and died. People who would work on her behalf. Sadly, at the moment, in the UK the people seemed to be overcome with apathy. Fewer than ever before voted. They said that politicians were all the same so why bother to vote. Democracy could see where they were coming from. She also knew that parts of the political process were unfair, and for her to be really safe they needed to change. Things were not looking good.

Fred Capitalism seemed to reach into every corner of life. Everything was about making money, greed is good, you can't be too rich or too thin: were the messages people were receiving with worrying regularity. No wonder there was so much unhappiness and stress around.

Democracy was beginning to feel that things were reaching a tipping point.

As if the banking crisis wasn't bad enough, Democracy began to see that another disaster was looming, a housing bubble. These were usually followed by a financial crash leading to terrible problems for many home-owners with mortgages. Fred Capitalism didn't care about people.

'It's the market correction,' he would say. 'My friend Big Business has made a lot of money.'

Democracy wondered if Fred Capitalism could change. Some politicians were now talking about trying to get good capitalism, by changing him.

'I don't really see that working,' said Democracy. 'Not while I am so weak.'

There is no doubt that Fred Capitalism was more ruthless than he used to be. Democracy thought it was because he believed he was the only game in town so that he could do what he wanted without check or hindrance. The sources of opposition that had previously held him in check, such as strong unions and socialism, were now much weaker. Democracy believed Fred Capitalism was now so strong that he was causing social, economic and even technological stagnation. His crony, Big Business, more or less controlled the media and even politics. They were all in thrall to Fred Capitalism.

'We are in a very dangerous situation,' Democracy said to her friends.

'Big Business is a more powerful player in the world that some Nation States and it is controlled by a few people who are accountable to no-one.'

'What can we do about it?' they asked.

Some of her friends were beginning to get anxious themselves.

'First we have to be aware of what is happening. They have used a very clever strategy, divide and rule,' said Democracy.

'What do you mean?' asked her friends.

'Well, blame all the problems on benefit scroungers and immigration, make them the scapegoats.'

Democracy didn't really understand why Fred Capitalism was so popular and doing so well everywhere. 'How can we get back to a fairer society?'

'It's no good asking economists,' she said to her friends. 'All they understand is making money.'

'Then ask other people; try philosophers, for a start.'

There she made more progress. Philosophers talked about "a decent society". Democracy started to think about what that would be. One thing was instantly clear to her. It wouldn't be based on worshipping the people who made the most money.

She knew she needed more information, so she thought she would try religious leaders to see what their take on things was. Some of them were well in with Big Business and Fred Capitalism. The Church had substantial assets and invested them to make money. However, there were some good signs. A few Church leaders were concerned about rising inequality and much keener on Democracy than Fred Capitalism. They also talked about morality and society.

Democracy was aware that one of the big problems for her was that people didn't really know what was going on, especially in Big Business. They didn't know how much corruption was taking place: tax evasion, lack of customer privacy, cheating, claiming taxpayers' money for work that had never been done. The list was long. Democracy could see that most people were busy trying to make ends meet and doing their best and didn't have the time or inclination to try and understand the real picture. How could they find out, anyhow? Only those on the inside really knew and they were generally more than happy with the status quo.

Democracy understood that she was weak and inexperienced and had powerful enemies. Only The People could change things, but they were in a state of apathy. One route to change, the politicians, were largely despised and regarded as a self-serving elite, so they were unlikely to provide an answer.

The only thing that kept her going was her belief that the idea of a common good was alive, not very well but still alive. She could see signs of it all around, in communities, in families, in workplaces, in charities, people who volunteered and gave time freely to others, like those on lifeboats who even risked their lives for others.

It seemed to Democracy that society needed to change, stop worshipping money and possessions and admiring crooks and money launderers. The stranglehold that Big Business and Fred Capitalism had on politicians and the media needed to be broken so that The People could see what was really happening before it was too late.

She was pinning her hopes on The People and the election. All of the political parties were in with Big Business, although perhaps not to the same degree. Some politicians had even tried to help Democracy by attempting to change the system. Sadly, that had not happened.

*

The election was over and once again there was a low turnout. Democracy was tired and disappointed. She stayed in bed the next morning and listened to the news on the radio. She felt too depressed to get up.

'Fred Capitalism is in danger of failing,' she heard. 'Extreme inequality will destroy him.'

She listened to the argument, which went along the following lines.

Fred Capitalism and Big Business need workers and if their pay and conditions get too bad, they will find ways to get back at their bosses. Fred Capitalism and The People need each other.

She sat up and had a long searching think about things and began to see that she could not live without Fred Capitalism and Big Business. She saw that when attempts had been made to take down regimes, for the sake of Democracy, they often failed. She thrived in countries where Fred Capitalism and Big Business helped create a good standard of living and all that came with it.

'I must stop fighting them,' she said.

'We will have to try and work together for the good of The People.'

She thought that there was no time to lose so she got in touch with them and offered to have a chat over a cup of coffee. To her surprise they agreed to meet her. During their chat they explained, 'We don't want to destroy you; we work best in places where you are alive and well.'

'I am more healthy when you are doing well, I suppose,' exclaimed Democracy.

'Some things are not good, there is too much greed and too little fairness and transparency for the good of The People,' she added.

To her amazement, Fred Capitalism and Big Business agreed.

'But it's the responsibility of The People,' they said. 'It's up to them to keep their eye on the ball and not just shrug their shoulders and complain. Everyone has a part to play in this.'

Democracy slowly sipped her coffee and realised that she had some thinking to do.

REALITY?
Power
Corporate greed. Wheels within wheels. It's who you know.
Politics
Hidden agendas. Eton and Oxbridge. It's class that counts.
Economics
Wishful thinking. Bankers and regulators. Blame it on globalisation.
Fairness
Get real. Trickledown effect? All in it together!
Poverty
Deep inequality. Generation after generation. It's your own fault.
Apathy
Don't bother. Democracy at risk. Maybe it's too late.

THE TIP OF THE ICEBERG

CHAPTER 1
ELLA

To mediate (verb), to intervene in a dispute to bring about a resolution

The six of us sat around the table and looked at each other warily. At least five of us had reason to be anxious or scared and that included me. I was grateful that the table was large. We all needed a bit of personal space. It was only ten o'clock in the morning, but it felt as if it had already been a long tiring day. I felt a mixture of terror and excitement. It's my first time as a lead mediator.

I had woken at six after a pretty awful night. It was still dark. Although I hadn't had much sleep, I had plenty of dreams. They were about losing my notes and forgetting what I wanted to say. Breakfast was out of the question; I just couldn't face it. There seemed no point in just sitting about fretting, so I dressed in my smart suit, packed my briefcase and set off for the mediation venue, an office in the city. In fact, I always arrive early at mediations. It's not just because

I'm nervous, although I am. It's part of being professional. It has taken a long time and a lot of effort to set up this mediation and I want to give it every possible chance. The other thing is that it is my first time as lead mediator. I've been an assistant dozens of times and at last I am the lead. So this is my big chance, and I want to make a good job of it, especially since I will be closely observed by Chas, who is much more experienced. So I'm hoping that we can get a resolution. A lot of work has preceded today's mediation. I've read pages of documents and made plenty of notes, so I think that I am on top of the issues. But there are always surprises; that's the most interesting part of the process, what pops up that's not in the paperwork.

I have spoken to both of the parties on the phone several times. Alexander Farr has been emailing me almost daily. I resisted an invitation to talk about the case over a drink. Not professional in my view. He has already made his position clear on the phone.

'I'll take him to the cleaners if he keeps on with this ridiculous case.'

However, he was more amenable to the idea of mediation than Jim Roberts, who explained quietly that legally he had a strong position and wanted financial compensation for his losses.

Chas, my fellow mediator, is like a man who has everything and is nevertheless up for more. If he was an animal, he would be a cat, one that had just had cream for breakfast and was anticipating a mouse for lunch. We talked together before the others arrived.

'It's your big day, Ella, hope you're up for it.'

I gave a withering smile and poured him a coffee, strong, with milk and no sugar.

'Ella, calm down, you nearly poured the coffee into my lap. You'll be fine. How do you want to play it? You're the lead today so it's your decision.'

I checked that I hadn't forgotten to wear my earrings, my lucky silver ones that my parents gave me for my 21st birthday. I always wear them when I have to do something important, especially if it's scary.

'I have spent sleepless nights deciding on the best way to conduct this mediation. Having spoken at length to both parties I think we can start with a joint meeting.'

Chas inclined his head slightly, more an acknowledgement than an agreement and I felt my stomach lurch. I fought a little battle with my nervousness and won narrowly. There was a noise in the corridor, so I got up to welcome the first arrivals.

'Stop fiddling with your earrings, Ella, they look fine.'

Jim Roberts, the claimant in the case, was the first to arrive. I had spoken to him on several occasions and his deep voice with a slight touch of a Welsh accent had a calming effect on me. His appearance did the same. He looked as if he spent a lot of time outdoors, his complexion weathered and his body strong and trim. We shook hands and his were slightly dry and rough. Compared with Chas, who looked sleek in his pinstriped suit and smelled of expensive aftershave, Jim was ruffled, dressed in chinos and leather jacket as befits an up-and-coming IT entrepreneur, and just smelled clean. I knew his back story, in brief, a clever creator of gadgets to delight the modern and seriously wealthy homeowner. If he was an animal, he would be a wolf.

'My lawyer has been delayed but will be here as soon as she can.'

My heart sank just a little. I feel more comfortable when everyone who should be around the table is there. I put on my smile and offered Jim a coffee. Chas sat down next to him and did what he does so well, which is oiling wheels.

The door opened and a small dark-haired man marched in followed by a tall man with rather long grey hair.

'Good morning, I'm Alexander Farr and this is my lawyer, Steven Ross.'

Jim gave a weak smile and Chas got up to shake hands and do some more wheel-oiling.

'We are just waiting for Mr. Roberts' lawyer and then we'll make a start. Meanwhile there is coffee and tea available.' I resisted the urge to give them animal identities since I didn't think it would be helpful.

We sat making small talk. Alexander shuffled his papers, and his lawyer wiped his glasses more than was strictly necessary.

Steven Ross got up and poured himself more coffee. He helped himself to two biscuits. Perhaps he eats when he is feeling unsure of himself. Jim appeared calm and sat quietly, although he glanced often at his mobile phone. I hoped that we wouldn't have to wait long since we needed to complete the mediation in a day.

When she did arrive, it was as if the light intensity in the room had increased. All the men sat up straighter, even Chas, who mostly preferred men. Jim stood up to introduce her. She was called Julia. It was going to be an interesting and challenging day. Jim gave Julia a coffee and I suggested that we start the first joint meeting in ten minutes, to give everyone a chance to get themselves ready.

I had already worked out the seating plan for this first joint session. We were using a round table. Chas was on my left, then Alexander with his lawyer next to him. To my right sat Jim with Julia on his right. When we were all settled, I made my opening remarks explaining that as mediators we were facilitators, we were not there to make judgments and that this mediation was voluntary. I also said that if anyone felt that the process was going nowhere, then they could bring it to an end and leave. I added that I hoped that that would not be the case. I emphasised that what was said during the mediation was confidential and could not be used elsewhere. After my introduction I asked if anyone had any questions. No-one did.

'Let's get on with it,' said Alexander.

'OK. Jim, as you are the claimant, will you or Julia make your opening statement. Please make it brief and it would be helpful if there were no interruptions at this point. There will be time for questions after the statements have been made.'

Jim's voice was vigorous as he outlined the substance of his claim.

'I am the CEO of a company which I set up with a few university friends a decade ago. We specialise in designing equipment for remote control of the home environment and over the last few years we have supplied such equipment to several companies, all of whom were delighted with it. I have letters to back this up. Some six months ago we were approached by Alexander Farr's construction company about supplying equipment for twenty-five luxury townhouses being built in Surrey. We agreed on the design of the equipment, and in due course supplied it, high-specification and expensive. When the invoice had not been paid in the agreed time, we contacted the buyer and were told that the stuff was not fit for purpose and that no money would be forthcoming.' At this point Jim's voice changed.

'The effect of this would be catastrophic for my company.' For a moment his voice became thin, and his eyes misted over.

Julia looked at him and smiled and he stiffened his back. When he next spoke, his voice was hard and cold.

'You have to pay. The equipment was made to your specifications and so cannot be used for other purposes. You know that. You entered into a contract; we delivered, so you should pay.' Julia touched his arm and he smiled.

While Jim had been speaking, Alexander had not taken his eyes off his face.

'Thank you, Mr Roberts. It is now your turn,' I said to Alexander Farr.

'My lawyer will present our case,' he said. Steven Ross looked at his open file and began his statement.

'Mr. Farr's construction company, RD Ventures, has been building high-end developments for some years, mainly in London and Surrey. One of the selling features of the properties are the remote-control facilities. The properties in question are extremely expensive, hence the sophisticated requirements of the remote-control systems which we specified with Mr Roberts. In construction work, all the components need to be available at the correct time otherwise the building will be held up, causing extra costs for the developer. This did not happen. The equipment did not arrive, and alternative suppliers had to be brought in. So Mr. Roberts' devices were surplus to requirements.' He looked at Alexander, who nodded his agreement.

During the statement, Jim looked rather taken aback and looked questioningly at Julia. She put her hand on his arm and gave it a squeeze.

'Are there any questions? Jim, do you want to respond?' He shook his head.

'Well, thank you both for that. We will now start the caucus sessions. Each party has a private room, and we will come and talk to you on your own and in confidence. Help yourself to coffee. We will start with you, Jim. Let us know when you are ready; we will be in the mediators' room.'

We all got up and left the room, helping ourselves to coffee and chocolate biscuits. I don't normally indulge but the stress of being the lead mediator was taking a lot of energy and a chocolate biscuit offered some comfort. We went to our three separate rooms.

'Well, that went OK,' said Chas. 'Nobody walked out. In fact, everybody was very calm considering how much money is at stake. What do you make of it? It all seems very straightforward. Julia seems to be there to provide emotional support for Jim, lucky chap. But there's usually more to these situations than meets the eye. Let's go and talk with Jim.'

CHAPTER 2
ELLA

I was surprised how much the task of facilitating the joint session had taken out of me. I felt the need to lie down in a dark room, and the day had only just begun. Maybe I wasn't cut out to be a mediator. I made myself put that thought behind me. So I asked Chas to run the meeting with Jim and Julia. He did his Cheshire cat grin.

'Happy to, Ella, I know it's knackering being the lead mediator when you start, but you'll get used to it.'

I was beginning to wonder if I wanted to. I think I take empathy too far.

He knocked on the door and we went into the room that Jim and Julia had been allocated. They were sitting very close together and seemed to be deep in mutual support. She had her arm around his shoulder and was stroking his back.

'Hope we aren't interrupting anything?' Chas said.

'It's OK,' said Julia as she moved away. 'Shall I pour us some coffee?'

Having already had several cups of strong coffee I felt hyped up as well as exhausted, so I declined, but Chas accepted and took a coffee to which he added plenty of milk. He really is like a cat. He can be kind when he chooses but he's got sharp claws, so I treat him with circumspection.

The room was small and gloomy, and I felt uncomfortable. We sat on either side of a small oblong table. I could smell Julia's perfume; it was the musky rather than the flowery type.

'What did you think about the opening joint session?' Chas asked. 'You can speak freely; what is said in this room remains here unless you agree for us to pass on something to the other party.'

'OK, what I expected really. Alexander is very cool, and his lawyer is even cooler. Don't be taken in by him, he's a very clever man.'

'Mmm,' said Chas, which I know meant that we should file that bit of information just in case it comes in useful.

Julia raised her eyebrows and gave Jim a warning look. She would be hard to ignore. Her painted nails were pistachio, the same colour as her obviously cashmere sweater. Striking! I could see Chas lapping her up.

'Tell me about your business, it sounds interesting.' Chas oiling the wheels again, he's really good at it. Jim relaxed into his explanation.

'I set it up a couple of years after leaving university. I did postgraduate work in MIT in Boston. That's where I came across the use of technology in controlling the home environment. It was quite a big thing in the US. It seemed to me that there would be a market back in the UK, especially for upmarket new builds in London.'

'I can see that,' said Chas. 'So then what did you do?'

'When I returned to the UK, I contacted a friend from university who was looking for a job and we agreed to set up the business. That was six years ago, and I have to say that we have been pretty successful so far.'

'You make it sound easy,' I said.

Julia laughed. 'He's just being modest; it was a lot of hard work and very stressful some of the time.'

'Julia is right, of course, we did have a few hiccups to start with, finding premises, recruiting engineers and so on, but it didn't take long to get up and running.'

'It must have cost a bit,' said Chas. 'Where did you get the money, was that a problem?'

Jim looked at Julia as if asking for approval. She nodded and Jim continued, 'Not really, my father had some spare money at the time, so he put it into the business.'

'Does that mean he is a shareholder?' I asked.

'No, he isn't. He is an MP, so he thought it better for all concerned to have no formal role, especially for him. He didn't want to break any rules.'

'Sounds pretty sensible,' said Chas.

The room seemed to be getting hotter.

'Where's the air conditioning control? Do you mind if we turn the temperature down?' asked Jim. He got up and fiddled with the controls then returned to his seat.

A good idea,' said Chas, then continued, 'so who are your clients, where do they come from?'

'Well, we do the usual stuff, we have a website, a marketing guy who is pretty good and we network, go to exhibitions, all that kind of thing.'

'I looked at your website, a pretty impressive list of big clients.'

'Yes, we've been lucky.'

Chas looked at me and indicated that I should pick up the discussion. We often did that, take it in turns to lead; it saved either of us getting too knackered. It was still only mid-morning and we had a long way to go. I kept looking at my watch. Time seemed to be dragging, I felt as if I was walking in treacle. I summoned up my small reserves of energy, since it was now down to me.

'So, you did postgraduate work at MIT; where were you at university?'

'At Imperial College, I studied electrical engineering.'

'That's pretty impressive, one of the best, so I believe.' I'm getting as oily as Chas!

Jim smiled. 'It's what I always wanted when I was at school. I was good at maths so that's what I wanted to be, a mathematician. After my first year at Imperial, I shifted sideways into electrical engineering. Good job I did, as you don't make much money being a mathematician.'

His voice sounded a bit different when he said that. You can tell a lot from voices. It sounded brash with undertones of sadness. I just filed that away for later.

'Is there anything else you want to tell us? How did you get the contract with Alexander?'

'You would need to ask our marketing man. The first I heard of it was an email from him saying that he wanted a meeting to discuss the possibilities. I had heard about his company so jumped at the opportunity.'

'So what went wrong?'

Jim sighed and looked at Julia. 'Do you think you could explain?'

'In a nutshell, Jim and his best engineer met with Alexander Farr and his house designer to discuss the project. They agreed that Jim would supply the home monitoring equipment for some luxury houses, a big and expensive project. On a later occasion there was a further meeting to fine tune the specifications and agree the costing and a delivery schedule. When the equipment was delivered according to plan, it was rejected.'

I looked at Jim.

'So what happened?'

'I don't know, but it has cost my company a huge amount of money which we can't afford to lose.'

'How much are we talking about here?'

I knew the amount only too well, having spent hours reading the documents. That's one of the things I enjoy the most, reading all the papers from both parties before the mediation.

'Four hundred thousand pounds. The equipment was made to a specification for a group of luxury properties and is of no use except in the properties they were designed for. If he doesn't pay up, then my business is in trouble. I really wanted to take them to court; I know I would win. I am sure that you are great mediators, so don't take it personally. They owe me a lot of money and I'd like to see them in court. They owe me and they should pay.' He banged the flat of his hand on the table.

'Let's stay calm, Jim,' Julia gently touched his arm. 'Your father doesn't want any publicity, so our options are limited.'

I've seen films of wolves howling at the moon. I felt as if that is what Jim wanted to do right then. Howl.

'You sounded a bit sad when you talked about changing your degree from maths to electrical engineering, or maybe I just imagined it.'

'No, you didn't imagine it, Ella. Can I call you Ella?'

'Of course.'

'I loved maths, thought I was good, so it was a bit of a blow when I realised that compared with the others I was just running to stand still. I don't like not being up in the front of the pack, so I decided to change tack. It worked out and I took a first. Actually, I find electrical engineering interesting, although maths will always be my first love.' He sighed quietly and looked away.

'Anyone fancy another coffee?' asked Chas. He uses drinks of any kind to oil the wheels.

Everyone nodded and Chas got up to get the drinks. I noticed that the room we were in was rather dark.

'How about some more light?'

'It's fine as it is, thanks,' said Julia.

While Chas was pouring the coffee, Jim looked at his mobile phone. Glaring would be a more accurate way of describing it.

'It's my damn father again. I need to speak to him; he just can't stay off my back, even today.' He pushed back his chair and picked up his phone as if it were something distasteful.

'I suppose I had better call him back, I'll just go outside.'

'Shall I come with you, Jim?'

'It's OK, Julia, I'll deal with it.'

Julia looked at her own phone and fiddled around with documents in her file. She was definitely lovely; a redhead with green eyes. Her skin was creamy and smooth with a voice to match. She hadn't said much yet and I was looking forward to listening to her say more.

In five minutes or so, Jim came back into the room. His outdoor-looking complexion was a new shade of red and I noticed Julia look at him with concern.

'Everything all right, Jim?'

'Just Dad wanting to know how we are getting on. I told him that I'd phone him this evening when all this is over.'

'Shall we carry on?' asked Chas.

Jim nodded.

'Had you done business with Alexander Farr before this contract?'

'No. When we met, he seemed familiar, and it turned out that we were at Imperial at about the same time. He was a year ahead of me, studying maths. He was bloody good, a little man with a big brain. Women seemed to like that; he had lots of women. He was like a magnet to them. Maybe because he was always buzzing with intellect. A bit sickening, really.'

He drank some coffee. It must have gone down the wrong way because he coughed and spluttered and stood up and left the room.

Chas looked at me and said, 'Mmm. Let's have a break now. We'll go and speak with the other party. OK with you, Ella?'

Jim came back into the room. 'Sorry about that, I think this is getting to me a bit.'

'Before we go to talk to the others, is there anything you want us to say to them?'

Jim looked at Julia.

'Not at the moment.'

CHAPTER 3
CHAS

I could see that Ella was struggling a bit, which isn't surprising. She takes the whole mediation thing very seriously and gets a bit too emotionally wound up in it. The first time of being a lead mediator is pretty challenging. It's important not to take sides, as we are supposed to be impartial and non-judgemental. I can tell that she really likes Jim, by the way she looks at him.

'Ella, do you feel up to leading the next session?'

'Yes, of course,' she said, so I gave her a smile which I hoped was encouraging.

We knocked on the door and went into the room allocated to Alexander Farr and his lawyer. Alexander put down the journal he was reading. I noticed that it was *The Economist*. Steven, his lawyer, was looking through his bundle of documents.

'What did you think of the joint session?' asked Ella.

Alexander frowned. 'As I expected, really. Jim always puts the blame somewhere else, it's never his responsibility.'

'Could you explain how you see it?' asked Ella.

'I sure can,' said Alexander. 'It's just as Steven said in the joint meeting. We agreed the spec. for the equipment and the time frame. It had to be ready so that it could be fitted at the appropriate stage in the building. It wasn't. It is a very expensive process to hold up the building schedule, so we had to find another supplier.'

'I would have thought that would be difficult to do at short notice,' I said. I know that Ella is not very clued up on technology.

'Actually, it was surprisingly easy. There are a growing number of companies who provide this sort of stuff. I thought that Jim would have been shrewd enough to realise that and deliver on time.'

'Do you know Jim well?'

'I wouldn't say that I know him well, but I know of him. We overlapped when we were at Imperial. I was a year ahead of him. We hung around with the same crowd for a short while. We used to go to the same parties; I suppose we knew the same people. You could say that we were fishing in the same pond.'

Ella looked slightly disapproving, so I gave her a look, just to warn her.

'How do you mean?' she asked, sounding innocent.

'Well, for a while we were involved with the same close friends.'

'Was that a problem?' asked Ella.

'Well, it did become a bit of a problem eventually. As usual, it was about a woman. I met her at a party. She was Jim's girlfriend; they sort of grew up together. It all seemed to be going well, as far as I could gather. Then as usual Jim's problems started to surface.'

'What sort of problems are you referring to?' said Ella in a cold voice.

'Jim always had a bit of a drink problem. I know lots of students drink too much but Jim was in a different league. Sometimes, not that often, he got very drunk. It happened on one occasion when we were at a party. Jim was too drunk to drive the woman home, so she came home in my car. We got talking, one thing led to another, and she left Jim and became my friend. It didn't last long, but I don't think Jim ever forgot or forgave me, or her for that matter.'

'That's understandable,' said Ella.

I gave her a firm look. Mediators must stay non-judgemental and impartial, and she was straying a bit.

'Yes of course it is,' said Alexander. 'I never forgave myself. I wasn't particularly keen on the woman, not in the way Jim was. The issue now is that Jim has problems remembering, handling and reconstructing the past in a way that he feels comfortable with. I can't forget it either. I have felt guilty ever since.'

Ella looked at me. I think she was asking for help on how to continue.

'These things happen,' I said consolingly.

'So, I tried to make amends; that's why I got in touch with Jim's company to offer the contract.'

'Did Jim know that?'

'Not to begin with, but he found out later.'

'How did he react?'

'What do you think? He's a proud man. He was bloody furious; it was like adding insult to injury.'

There is usually a point in mediations when the unknown factors start to emerge. The presenting problem is sometimes only the tip of the iceberg. This was the situation here, it seemed.

'So, then what happened?' asked Ella in a small, controlled voice.

'Jim told me that I wasn't his favourite client, but that business is business. So I thought everything would be fine. Well, not exactly fine, but OK.'

Alexander drew a deep breath. 'I was obviously wrong.' There was a long silence.

Ella is good with silences, whereas I find them difficult.

'Have you kept in touch with Jim since university days?' I asked, to break the silence.

'No, I haven't seen him for years, but I knew about this business of his from his father.'

'The MP?'

'Yes, I came across him in planning committees.'

'Jim's father has done some lobbying for a construction group that builds hospitals and other status projects,' said Steven.

Ella frowned in disapproval but at least kept her mouth shut.

'He makes sure that people know about the stuff that Jim does; it's used increasingly in hospitals, especially private ones.'

'So, what was your reason for employing Jim?'

'As I said, I always felt guilty about taking the woman that Jim was so keen on. I suppose I wanted to make amends so that I could stop feeling guilty. It really wasn't my finest hour when I started a relationship with Jim's woman.'

Alexander twisted the gold and diamond ring on his little finger.

'I felt tarnished and that's not a good feeling. I thought giving Jim the contract would make me feel better.'

'Did it?' said Ella, rather aggressively, I thought.

'For a while it did. I hoped that we would be able to smooth over the past. I didn't think that we would be friends; we are much too different in personality for that, but business colleagues. After we signed the contract, we shared a drink or two, as part of a crowd, not just us.'

'So what do you think happened? Why didn't the equipment arrive on time?'

'Who knows, perhaps Jim was getting his own back. I gather he was very cut up about the loss of the woman.'

'Is there anything you want us to say to Jim?' asked Ella.

Alexander sat very still and looked out of the window at the luminous sky.

'As I've said, I am sorry that it happened. I would like to apologise for taking advantage of the situation and causing Jim such a lot of distress. I'm not generally an unkind person but that was an unkind act which I deeply regret.'

In my years as a mediator, I have been surprised and impressed at the power of a genuine apology for all concerned. So I felt that we had taken a positive step forward.

'OK, we'll go back and talk to Jim and tell him what you just said. It may make a difference.' Ella and I got up to leave.

'This whole wretched business has been hanging over me like a black cloud. I hope we can clear it up.'

CHAPTER 4
ELLA

I was now starting to feel hungry. No breakfast and just a few biscuits so far today; my stomach was telling me that it was lunch time. I looked at my watch and it was 12.30 pm.

'Shall we have lunch before we speak again with Jim?'

'Sounds good to me,' said Chas.

We went out into the main reception area, where fresh tea and coffee and plates of sandwiches were laid out. I was glad that each party had lunch in separate rooms to give us some time out. I knew that we all needed it.

'I'll go and tell them that lunch is available,' said Chas. 'I'll see you in the mediators' room, Ella.'

I chose my sandwiches and poured fresh coffee, then went to the mediators' office to be joined by Chas. We both tucked into our sandwiches in silence. It was a relief to feel hungry again.

'How do you think its going?'

'OK,' said Chas. 'We are making progress. I am surprised that Alexander is prepared to apologise, but good for him.'

We had all agreed that half an hour for lunch was long enough.

'Are you all right to run the next session, Ella?'

'Yes, I think so. At least we have something to offer Jim.'

We knocked on the door of the room occupied by Jim and Julia. When we entered, they quickly moved apart. She kept her eyes on his face while we explained that Alexander wanted to apologise for his behaviour when they were students at Imperial College. I had written down his exact words, with his permission, and read them out to Jim. As I was reading, I could feel my heart rate increase as I had a moment of doubt. Maybe this would make things worse. When I finished there was silence. It seemed to last a long time. I could hear the traffic outside, but it sounded as if I were hearing it through cotton wool.

Jim could never look pale, he was too much the outdoor weathered type, but there was a look of distress on his face, and I felt that he was vulnerable. I had to resist offering him some kind of comfort. Clearly, Julia could see it too. She put her hand over his and gently squeezed it. I held my breath as I waited for his response. He seemed to be making an effort to compose himself before he replied.

'That was all a long time ago, of course I was angry at the time. I'm glad he's apologised but you can't undo what happened. Life has moved on, his behaviour had bad consequences for me.'

The room went quiet. I can cope with silences so long as they don't last too long.

Jim looked at Julia.

'I'm in a good place now, so let's just get on with things. Is he prepared to pay for the equipment that he commissioned from my company?'

'We haven't discussed that yet. Alexander was clear that first of all he wanted to apologise for his behaviour. I don't think he appreciated how upset you would be, and he has felt guilty ever since. Can we tell him that you accept his apology? Then we can talk about the money.'

Jim and Julia agreed, and Chas and I went back to begin the financial discussions with Alexander and his lawyer. The fact that Jim had accepted his apology seemed to have a positive effect on Alexander.

'I wish I had been able to do that a long time ago, it feels as if a weight has been lifted from me. Let's get this all sorted out.'

He turned to his lawyer.

'How much is Jim asking for?'

'Four hundred thousand pounds.'

'Is that the final amount?'

'Yes, I believe so. Perhaps the equipment could be sold to another developer?'

'Unlikely, as it was made to a very particular specification.'

'Shall we offer half that?' asked the lawyer.

'No, I want this brought to a conclusion today. I agree to pay him what he is asking for.'

'Can we just have in word in private, Mr. Farr?' His lawyer looked uncomfortable at the way things were going.

'No, there is no point in discussing it. I have made up my mind. Tell Jim that I agree to his demands. Can you do the necessary so that this can all be sewn up this afternoon?'

I looked at Chas. He nodded.

'If you are quite sure that it's what you want, then we can do that. Shall I go and tell Jim about your decision?' He nodded.

When I explained what the outcome of the mediation was to Jim, his response was not what I had expected. Rather than relief and pleasure, he looked as if he was going to cry as he slumped down in his seat. Julia looked at him with surprise and then annoyance.

'What more do you want, Jim? This is the best you could get, think how pleased your father will be.'

'He's done it again,' he said. 'He always manages to make me feel disempowered.'

CHAPTER 5
ELLA

When I got back to my flat, I treated myself to a large glass of Muscadet. My first lead mediation had been successful. We had an agreement. The papers had been drawn up and signed by all parties. I could see that Chas was pleased.

'Well done, Ella, you worked hard,' he said, and gave me a hug. It wasn't yet four o'clock when we left the offices. As soon as the papers were signed, Jim and Julia left. I noticed that Jim didn't look at Alexander. Sometimes, when we reach an agreement, we invite the parties to shake hands. There was no chance that Jim was going to shake hands with anybody. He slunk out of the room, his lips tightly closed. He looked like the loser rather than the winner.

I wrote up my mediation report and thought about the dynamics of the personal relationships of the parties. It had certainly been an interesting case. As often happens, the presenting issues were just the tip of the iceberg. I was learning that the need for self-esteem is very powerful and can often be a factor in dispute situations. Chas and I had agreed to meet the next morning to wrap up the case paperwork. It was also his role to give me feedback on how I had done as the lead mediator.

We met at my favourite coffee shop, which I liked mainly because of the walls, which looked as if they were lined with bookshelves filled with books. It was only wallpaper, but I liked it anyway. As is my wont, I arrived early, ordered my one-shot-only coffee and took it upstairs to the book-lined room. Since we were planning a serious discussion, I chose to sit at a table rather than on the shabby chic sofas. Chas was late. He never is for mediations but can't seem to be punctual for anything else. He eventually joined me with his two-shot coffee and a cake and his computer bag slung over his shoulder.

'Good morning, Ella, trust you slept better last night?'

'Yes, thank you, although I kept thinking about it.'

'I don't think one ever forgets one's first lead mediation. I can still remember mine although it was years ago. The office is dealing with the paperwork from yesterday, including of course the bills to Jim and Alexander. So how do you think it went, Ella?'

I had been anticipating this question, to the extent of preparing my answer. We had a general discussion about the case which was made more difficult by the arrival of two young mothers with small children. They seem to use the coffee shop as a crèche.

'There's just one thing, Ella, which I need to talk to you about.'

I sipped my coffee, which was cold and tasted bitter. I could feel my heart rate increasing. I hate this sort of feedback.

'Only one?' I said, trying to lighten things.

'Yes, don't worry, it's not really serious. It's just that I thought that you were getting emotionally involved.'

I put my coffee cup down just in case my hand started to shake. Because I knew he was right.

'You seemed to be very drawn to Jim?' he went on.

He put it as a question, or that's how I picked it up.

'I know what you mean,' I said. 'He is the sort of man that I find very attractive, and I did feel for him, I felt that he was vulnerable.'

'Well, you know that the mediator's role is to be impartial and non-judgmental so getting in too close is just not on.'

'I know that. I don't usually have such strong reactions to people, especially when I have just met them.'

'OK, that's all I wanted to say. Just be on your guard and try and be detached.'

We sat there chatting for about half an hour and I felt my heart rate go back to normal. All in all, the mediation had gone rather well, and Chas said that he would give positive feedback about my performance to our mediation panel. He even said that he was looking forward to working with me again. After he left, I walked around the shops and as a treat bought myself a silver chain and two novels.

*

I had planned to spend the afternoon at home relaxing, which for me takes the form of reading, especially novels. So I made a cup of coffee and settled into my armchair by the window, so that the light comes in over my shoulder, ideal for reading. After a few pages I put the book down. I would have to start again. The words had just gone into my head and then straight back out again. I felt as if I was waiting for something. I went over the morning's talk with Chas. He's very perceptive. When mediating with him I have often been impressed by his almost sixth sense of what people are feeling, even when they are trying to hide it. Especially when they are trying to hide it. He was spot on about me. I was particularly moved by Jim; just thinking about him affected me.

My mobile phone pinged. To my surprise it was a message from Alexander Farr.

'Can we meet? I need to talk to you.'

I decided to delay replying. In most cases after the mediation, the participants don't want to see us again. They are usually glad that it's all over and want to get on with their lives. Once the case is over, there is no legal reason why we shouldn't meet but it's never happened before. I thought about it and my curiosity got the better of me, so I called Alexander. He said that he didn't want to discuss it over the phone, so we arranged to meet at my local pub in the evening.

When I got to the pub, Alexander was already sitting at a table with a pint of beer. It hadn't become a refurbished gastro pub so there were still swirly carpets and curtains which made it easy to have a quiet conversation. Alexander got me a large glass of dry white wine.

'Thank you for agreeing to meet,' he smiled. 'I appreciate that it's not usual, but you seemed to be a sympathetic sort of person, so I thought I would risk asking.'

'It's not about the mediation, is it?'

'No, that's all over and done with. It's about Jim.'

Why does even the mention of his name disturb me?

'Is he all right?' I hoped that my sudden anxiety didn't show.

'I've heard a few disturbing things.'

'Who from?'

'I've got a lot of contacts in the property development world. Apparently, Jim's dad has disappeared.'

When I get anxious, I try to control my breathing, to keep it slow and regular, but it didn't seem to be working so I drank some of my wine while I collected my thoughts.

'He was around yesterday.'

'What makes you think that?'

'He phoned Jim during the mediation.'

'That could have been from anywhere. He should have been at some important development meeting yesterday and he didn't show.'

'There could be plenty of reasons for that.'

'Yes, that's true, but no one has been able to reach him. It's quite unlike him. He takes his responsibilities very seriously and I know that this was an important meeting. He was opposing the development of a high-rise block of flats, and this was the agenda for the meeting. It would have taken something serious to keep him away.'

'So why are you telling me, what can I do?'

'Well, I got the sense that you liked Jim and he could probably do with a bit of support.'

I could feel my face getting hot. How embarrassing that even Alexander had noticed. Chas was right, I need to be more impartial, or I'd never be a good mediator. I felt a bit disappointed in myself.

'I'll give it some thought. Why are you so concerned?'

'I just can't totally forgive myself for the hurt I caused Jim.'

CHAPTER 6
ELLA

That night I didn't get much sleep. I kept dreaming about Jim and Alexander. Every time I woke up, and there were lots of times, I went over what Alexander had told me. By the early hours I had made up my mind that I would contact Jim. Chas wouldn't really approve so I just wouldn't tell him, at least not at the moment. After I had made my decision, I did get some sleep.

After breakfast, I looked through the mediation documents and located Jim's number. I managed to wait until mid-morning before I called. I settled down at my desk with a cup of coffee to make the call. Since I had spent ages working out what to say I checked my script. I could hear it raining on the Velux window. Just ringing his number made my heart race. Perhaps he wouldn't answer.

'Jim Roberts, how can I help you?'

'Hello Jim, it's Ella. How are you?'

Jim sighed.

'I'm OK, just a bit worried about my father. He didn't turn up for an important meeting a few days ago and my mother doesn't know where he is. Look, I don't want to talk about this over the phone.' I held my breath. 'So could we meet? I need to talk about it to someone.'

I forgot about my prepared script and agreed. I expect that I sounded rather keen, despite trying to stay cool.

We arranged to meet in a coffee shop that afternoon.

The time passed slowly until just before three o'clock, the time I had planned to set off. I dressed casually, but with great care. I felt like a teenager again, nervous before a date.

The venue had been chosen by Jim. It was a coffee shop in a department store, not my favourite. But at least it was on the top floor and had lovely views. Well, it would have been a good view except it was raining. Jim was already there because I had deliberately arrived late. The leather jacket and chinos looked great, and his smile seemed genuine and warm. He ordered a coffee for me and, with my encouragement, told me what he was concerned about.

'As you know, my father is an MP. For the last six months or so he has been involved in a planning application for a high-rise block of flats in his constituency. There has been opposition to the plans and my father has been a high-profile lead in this. He has been lobbied by some of his constituents, who claim that first, the flats will overlook a school play area and second, that building them will undermine an old cinema which is a listed art deco building. He has received a lot of publicity about this, some of it bad, and is now getting unpleasant emails, some of which are threatening. He wasn't that bothered; he said that it isn't unusual because the government sometimes makes decisions which some people don't like.'

'One of the downsides of being an MP, I suppose,' I said, with what I hoped was a sympathetic voice.

'Yes, well according to my mother he didn't come home three nights ago, and she is starting to worry about him.'

'Has he been in touch?'

'Yes, by text with her and if you remember he contacted me during the mediation. I didn't know that he had disappeared then.'

'What did he talk to you about?'

'The mediation and how it was going. He was keen on the mediation because he didn't want a court case with all the publicity.'

'Well, that's understandable. That's the other downside of public life, publicity.'

We had settled into our discussion, and I confess that I was enjoying the fact that Jim was giving me a hundred per cent of his attention. I felt very alert and alive. Physical attraction has that effect on me.

'How do you think I can help you, Jim?'

'I don't know at the moment. Your colleague, Chas, I bet he has a lot of high-level connections. Could he do anything?'

I felt that sudden sinking feeling of disappointment. He just wanted to use me, as a way in to more influential people.

'Oh, you don't need Chas,' I said without thinking.

'OK,' he said slowly. 'Can you get me information about the building developers? If we knew who was involved, it might give me some idea of where to start.'

'I expect I can, I do have some contacts myself,' I surprised myself by saying.

'That would be great, Ella, I would really appreciate that.'

I smiled, although I was beginning to feel a bit uneasy about what I was getting into. My next mediation wasn't for a few weeks, so I had some spare time. I expect that I can do research as well as anyone else.

Jim drained his cup of coffee and stood up to put on his leather jacket. As I was already only too well aware, he had a great body, strong and slim. I think he knows it and is aware of my attraction to him. I don't sense that he is particularly attracted to me, well, not yet, anyway.

'I have to get back to work, thanks, Ella. Why don't you ring me when you find out anything useful?'

'Will do.'

I stood up and we shook hands. It felt a bit awkward. As Jim left the room, I noticed that a few people watched him; they were all women!

CHAPTER 7
ELLA

It was raining harder when I left the coffee shop. Since I like rain, I decided to walk home. The cobbled high street was slippery, and I was so preoccupied thinking about Jim that I slipped once or twice and caught myself just in time. When I got to the river near my flat, I paused to watch the ducks, snuggling into the river bank. There was no one to feed them. It was too wet and windy. By the time I got home I was soaked through, so I changed into dry clothes and poured myself a glass of wine. A bit early, but it was a special occasion. It was the beginning of something with Jim.

I like reading the bundle of mediation papers and I like research, so I switched on my laptop and made a start. Because I was doing it for Jim, I relished it and made good progress. I found the planning application on the council website and the information about the developers. It was a consortium of three companies. I looked up the three companies and one of them was RD Ventures. It rang a bell. Then I remembered that it was Alexander Farr's construction company. I sipped my wine and started to make some notes. This was getting interesting. I had not heard of the other two companies. When I researched them on the web, I found out that one was Danish, and the other was a company registered in the British Virgin Islands with UK offices in Bridport in Dorset.

Their websites gave information about other completed developments. They appeared impressive and I noticed that several of them had used Jim Roberts as a consultant for the installation of remote-control IT systems. I can't explain it, but I felt a little trickle of apprehension as I read this. I made more notes and poured myself another glass of wine. I turned off the laptop and sat in my reading armchair to think. Chas talks a lot about 'the tip of the iceberg'. I think he might be right in this case. When I had enough of trying to make sense of things, I picked up the novel I was reading to take my mind onto other matters. It was a good strategy and I slept surprisingly well.

I woke up the next morning with the sun streaming into my bedroom. After the rain, the world looked fresh through my Velux windows, and I felt something verging on happiness. My late-night thoughts about Jim and his dad had just gone around in circles and I realised that I just didn't have a clue about what to do next. A more experienced head was required; I would have to overcome my reluctance and speak to Chas. He had been around the block a few times, as the saying goes, and maybe could give me some ideas. I allowed myself a cup of tea and a slice of crusty toast. Fortified, I called him on his mobile.

'Can we meet for lunch or just a coffee if you are too busy? I need to pick your brains.'

'Of course, I have a free day today so lunch would be fine.' I felt relief wash over me and we agreed a time and a venue. As usual Chas was late, only ten minutes, which was good for him. We ordered our pizzas and some sparkling water.

'OK Ella, what's this about? Let me guess, it's to do with Jim, I bet.'

I felt my face go hot and sipped some of my water to help me regain some composure.

'Yes, I saw him yesterday. You know his dad has disappeared. He wondered if I could help in some way.'

'I told you, Ella, that you were getting emotionally involved here, it's not a good idea. You know very little about Jim and his dad, it could be trouble. Why don't you stay out of it?'

'I don't know. I expect that you are right. I do like him and want to help.'

'You might be taking on a lot more than you realise. I think that you should stay well out of it.'

'Out of what exactly?'

'It sounds to me as if there is a whiff of corruption here.'

'What do you mean?'

'From what you have told me so far it could be that the issues around the developers and the planning permission may have something to do with it. It's a very brave person who stands in the way of developers and their ambitions. From what you have told me that is what Jim's dad is doing.'

Although I had only eaten half of my pizza, I no longer felt hungry. My concern must have shown on my face.

'Don't worry, Ella. I expect that he'll turn up soon. There will probably be a simple explanation. If he hasn't turned up in a few days, I'll have a word with some of my contacts to see what I can find out. Now eat your pizza like a good girl.'

I smiled. Chas can be very kind. He had some shopping to do so we left the restaurant with an arrangement to speak in a few days. Although I had had doubts about involving Chas, I felt that I had made the right decision. It felt more comfortable having him keeping an eye on me.

That evening I did some research about corruption. It was a subject that I had hardly ever considered. Although during mediations I had come across broken contracts, disputes about money, I had not seen anything that I would have described as corruption. It crossed my mind that perhaps I was naïve. So I looked it up on the internet.

> *Corruption (Wikipedia) is a form of dishonest or unethical conduct by a person with a position of authority often to acquire personal benefit. Corruption may include many activities including bribery and embezzlement though it may involve practices that are legal in many countries.*

Although there seemed to be a lot of corruption going on in the world, the UK hardly got a mention. Maybe that was because we were so good at it, more subtle and restrained. Some forms of corruption, for example, bribery and dishonest behaviour, were seen as part of business and professional life. Nobody took it seriously. It was often done behind closed doors, so few people knew the details and those who did were so used to it that they regarded it as normal business practice. I had a lot to think about, which gave me another sleepless night.

CHAPTER 8
CHAS

When Ella gets her teeth into something she is like a terrier dog, she won't let go. This is what is happening with the Jim episode. She called me today to tell me that Jim's dad is still missing. She is a good, well-meaning woman although she goes off at a tangent from time to time. I've been persuaded to meet with Jim and Julia, and Ella, of course, to see if I can be of any help.

The meeting has been arranged in a pub suggested by Jim. It's the other side of town from where I live, so I hope it doesn't go on for long since I have my own social life to nurture and have arranged to have a late supper with George, my latest love interest. So I agreed to meet at six o'clock. That should give us plenty of time. I never arrive exactly on time, except for important things like mediation. So it was about six-fifteen when I walked into the bar of the Red Parrott. It was an old London pub, still with its stained glass in the windows and door, and a long bar with a mirror behind it, my kind of place, so well chosen, Jim. They were already sitting at a table with a bottle of white wine and four glasses. I prefer gin and tonic but accepted a glass of wine.

'Thank you for coming,' said Julia, in her low velvety voice.

'I hope I can help,' I smiled. She made me really want to, somehow.

'I understand that Ella has explained the situation,' said Jim.

'Yes, she has. Have you any more information?'

'None, and my mother is getting rather worried. This has never happened before.'

'Have you any idea where he might be? Does he have a reason to go AWOL?'

'On the contrary, he was all prepared to speak at the planning meeting, to oppose the high rise. He had been preparing for it for a while and was keen to get on with the process.'

'Could his absence have anything to do with that planning meeting?' asked Ella.

'I don't know, I suppose it's a possibility.'

'Well, the most important task is to find out where he is and to ensure that he is all right.'

'Yes, it is,' said Jim in a small voice. 'I'm starting to worry myself. It's unusual for him to be out of contact. He usually has too much contact for my liking.'

No one spoke for a few minutes. I noticed that the bottle of wine was empty.

'I'll get us some more drinks. Another bottle of white wine?' They nodded.

When I got back from the bar with the bottle of wine, they looked at me expectantly as if I would have the plan for what to do next.

'Thank you, Chas, not just for the wine but for helping us,' said Julia.

I sighed. I had been drawn in despite my misgivings.

'I do have some contacts that may be able to help us find him. If you agree, I will talk to them. Of course, they will want to talk to you, Jim, and also your mother.'

'Yes of course, the sooner the better,' said Jim. 'I suppose this is going to be expensive?'

I thought of the four hundred thousand pounds that he had just got from Alexander.

'Not very, I'm sure you can afford it. They charge per day and their expenses.'

Julia put her hand on Jim's arm.

'It's your dad: we mustn't even think about the money.'

'Of course, you are right. I'm just finding this all very stressful.'

'What happens next?' asked Ella. I knew that she desperately wanted to be part of this adventure.

'I will arrange a meeting with my contact and you, Jim. I am away at a mediation in the next few days so Ella will be the go-between. Is that OK with you, Ella?'

'Of course,' she said. Her eyes were wet and shining. She was just like a determined and enthusiastic terrier.

I keep my word, usually, so the next day I called ex-brigadier Peter North and outlined the situation. I have known Peter since we were at public school. We kept in touch during our university days and even after, when we went our separate ways, he into the army and I into the law. He retired from the army a few years ago and now does freelance security work. We meet up from time to time for a drink and a catch-up. He doesn't talk about his work much, but from what he has said it's not far from what we need now. I outlined the situation and asked if he could help. He agreed, as I knew he would. Over the years we have done each other a few favours. I gave him Ella's contact details as I have too much on to give it any more time and I know that she is keen to help Jim. We agreed to meet up in a couple of weeks so that he could keep me in the picture. I am concerned that Ella doesn't get too involved in this. It may not be good for her.

CHAPTER 9
ELLA

A chap called Peter contacted me. He is a friend of Chas and is going to try and find Jim's dad, so I set up a meeting with him and Jim. I included myself, of course. Jim said that discretion was important, so we agreed to meet at his office after work, when all the other staff had left. On the occasions that I am lucky to meet Jim I always take particular care to look as good as I can. Since it was after work it was OK to wear black, I thought. It suits me, or so I've been told. Jim's office was a Tube ride away and I live a good ten minutes' walk from the station, but I wore my high heels although I knew that my feet would be tender by the time I got to the meeting. I am always amazed at the lengths I go to when I fancy somebody! It was raining when I left my flat. Since I like the rain, it put me in a good mood. It was easy to find the office. Jim's company office was rented space in a modern office block. It was well chosen; lights went on automatically when you entered a room and I presume went off when you left it. The furnishings were simple and the place uncluttered. I was surprised; I had imagined Jim to be more into natural wood and fabrics, not plastic and stainless steel.

'Thanks for this, Ella.'

'Still no news from your father?'

'No, I'm really scared about what might have happened to him.'

The buzzer on the door to the office suite indicated that Peter had arrived, and Jim and I got up to welcome him.

'Hello, you must be Jim and Ella, pleased to meet you both. Call me Peter.'

I felt safer just having him in the room. It wasn't just that he looked strong and fit; lots of people have that quality. Sometimes I actually find it threatening. Not on this occasion, because he had a kind face. We sat around a small conference table and Peter took a small notebook and pen from his pocket.

'I have a pretty good memory, but I prefer to take a few notes; not on a computer. This is more secure.'

Jim must have looked sceptical.

'Nobody can read my writing,' he said with a chuckle.

'Jim, have you any idea where your father might be? Has he done this before?'

'Not in the same way. He does go off on his boat sometimes. He says it takes his mind off everything else, so it's good for getting away from all the stress, or so he says.'

'I can see that, I do a bit of it myself, for the same reasons. Where does he keep the boat?'

'In a marina in Lymington on the south coast.'

'Could he have gone there, do you think?'

'I suppose so.'

'I suggest that I check it out. Have you got any other thoughts about where he might be?'

'Not really, it's not like him to miss one of these planning meetings. He was getting well stuck into opposing the development.'

Peter stood up and walked slowly towards the window. It was just getting dark outside, and I could see his reflection in the window. He turned around slowly and looked at Jim.

'Is your father being threatened? Developers don't always wear kid gloves, especially when their plans are being thwarted.'

'He's not said anything, but I suppose he could be.' Jim's voice went quiet and small.

'If you want me to help you need to tell me what you know, Jim,' Peter said.

I smiled at Jim in what I hoped was a supportive and encouraging way. I don't think he noticed. He looked out of the window. His anxious face was reflected in it. He seemed to be in a world of his own.

'I just hope that it has nothing to do with me.'

'How could it?' Peter asked in a surprisingly gentle voice.

'Well, I have made a few mistakes in my business career and Dad has always got me out of the mess I've made.'

'Do you think this could be relevant to your father's disappearance?'

'Christ, I hope not, I have caused him enough problems.'

'Is there any trouble at the moment, Jim?'

'I suppose you could say that there is. I've signed a contract that I can't fulfil. I've taken the first payment and used it to pay a debt I had. So now I don't have the funds to buy the equipment I need to do the job. I could be taken to court and have a hefty fine, as well as lawyers' bills to pay. It would wipe me out.' He looked as if he wanted to howl to the moon. I just wanted to hold him tight and tell him that it would all be all right. The thought of the £400,000 from Alexander flashed through my mind. I told myself that it wasn't my job to mention it.

'Does your father know about this?'

'Yes, I asked him for help.'

'What sort of help?'

'I asked if he could use his influence to get them off my back.'

'And...'

'He was furious, and he had every right to be, but after he had calmed down, he said he would see what he could do.'

'You are very lucky to have a father like that,' I said. I couldn't help saying it.

'It's not because of me, I think he despises me, he does it for my mother.'

Peter had not taken any notes but now he picked up his pencil.

'Give me the details of the marina and the berth information and boat name. I'll drive down tomorrow and see if he's there.' He wrote down the information and got up to leave. Jim escorted him out of the office and thanked him with some humility. When he came back into the room I stood up and held out my arms. Everyone needs a hug sometimes. Especially me.

CHAPTER 10
PETER

Even during the autumn, the roads to the south coast are busy. I got to the marina in Lymington by mid-morning. I enjoy these mild October days, and envied those who had enough time and money to be able to spend their weekdays on the water, or even just sitting on their boats, sipping their coffee and catching up on the news. The marina office told me the number of Mr. Roberts' mooring and volunteered the information that he had been away for a few days but was expected back later today. So I settled down to wait. I found a seat with a sea view and poured myself a coffee from my flask and opened my tin of biscuits. Not quite as nice as sitting on a boat but pleasant enough. The Yarmouth to Lymington ferry came and went four times. Other than that, there was very little movement of boats despite the seemingly perfect sailing weather. One yacht came into the Lymington River; I got out my binoculars to have a better look. On board was a man by himself. The yacht slowly moved towards the vacant place belonging to Mr. Roberts MP. If I hurried, I could be on the pontoon and offer to take his ropes, a helpful gesture to a single-handed sailor.

Mr Roberts, although a competent sailor, clearly appreciated my assistance. He looked tired.

'Had a good trip?'

We made the usual small talk while we made the boat secure.

'Can I have a word, sir? I'm here on behalf of your family. They have been worried about you.'

'You had better come aboard; I could do with a cup of coffee.'

He moved wearily about the boat, turning on the gas, filling the kettle. His eyes were red either from the wind or from crying. We sat opposite each other with our coffees on the table between us.

'I've had a bloody awful time but running away doesn't resolve anything. Has Jim told you what's been going on? Or is he too ashamed?'

'I think it would be better coming from you. Why didn't you turn up for the planning meeting?'

'Because if I had, Jim would be in court, and I can't contemplate that.' I stayed silent and just looked at him sympathetically.

'Jim has been a fool. He gets carried away and puts in estimates for jobs that are totally unrealistic. OK, so he gets the job, then he can't deliver. He doesn't bloody learn.'

He told me with a catch in his voice that he had agreed to stay away from the meeting to prevent Jim being taken to court by the construction company.

'Jim has been worried about you.'

'It's not the first time this has happened. I'm an executive director for the latest company he has let down, which makes it embarrassing. They are part of a consortium that has put in the bid for development. I expect he told you that for once I'm against it.' I raised my eyebrows.

'My wife is a governor of the school which is affected by the plans. Obviously, she's against the development. It puts me in a difficult position.'

He must have sensed my next question.

'With the way things are going I may well lose my seat at the next election. I have to do something, I'm too young to retire and I need money. I have been offered a job with the construction consortium when my political career comes to an end.'

My heart sank. I remembered reading about these arrangements, the so called "revolving door".

Revolving door. Wikipedia

In politics, a revolving door is a situation in which personnel moves between roles as legislators and regulators, on the one hand, and members of the industries affected by the legislation and regulation on the other, analogous to the movement of people in a physical revolving door.

I knew it happened; I had come across it a couple of times during my work. I felt uncomfortable but it was none of my business and it hadn't happened yet.

'What are you going to do now? You can't stay away much longer without questions being asked.'

He got up; there was just about enough headroom in the cabin and looked out of the hatch. It was still a lovely day but when he turned back his face looked bleak.

'I'll phone my wife and Jim. I'll get back to work and see what happens. I expect I can kiss goodbye to working for the construction consortium, I just hope that's the only consequence. At least my wife will be pleased.'

I debated for a moment whether to tell him the outcome of the planning meeting. He had a right to know.

'I've heard that because there was less opposition at the planning meeting, the development has been agreed.'

'So my wife won't be pleased about that. It seemed that it was either pleasing her or protecting Jim. I hope I made the right choice.'

I held my tongue. Platitudes were the last thing he needed. He seemed like a good bloke to me.

'I'm glad that you are OK, Mr Roberts. If I can be of help any time, just let me know.'

CHAPTER 11
CHAS

I'm up to speed with the reappearance of Mr. Roberts MP, thanks to Ella. I encourage her to keep me in the picture. She's mad about Jim and I fear that she is getting more involved than is wise. Sometimes I think that I've forgotten what it's like to be young and in love. We have mediation in a couple of weeks, so I hope she isn't getting too distracted.

I'm very busy working with the government trying to promote mediation. It could save a lot of court time and money. There seems to be some resistance to the idea, so I'm putting a lot of effort into networking to try and win hearts and minds. Hence my acceptance of an invitation to a reception at the Royal Academy. There will be lawyers to engage with, and also quite a few MPs. If there's free champagne, they will turn up. I don't think we will make any progress without their help. The invitation was for me and partner. I'm getting involved with a younger man. It's not serious and he's not the sort to take to this do. He thinks pictures are an affectation and doesn't like politicians. So I'm going by myself.

Piccadilly station is heaving with lovely young men in smart suits going home from work. Hope the evening won't be too boring. By the time I get to the Royal Academy, slightly late as usual, most of the guests have arrived, judging by the din. There is a queue for the cloakroom and the usual security hassle so by the time I reach the first-floor main gallery, I'm gasping for a glass of champagne. These are not priceless works of art, so we are allowed to take our glasses into the galleries. The rooms are hot and very crowded so that there is a sort of shuffle to move around. I'm not particularly interested in paintings, I'm here to network, but it's difficult when there are so many people.

I thought I would know more people, but my barrister friends are nowhere to be seen. The only person I recognise is Peter, along with a few ex-service colleagues. He's a good man, so I smiled and waved. We pushed our way through the throng of people and met by the gallery doorway. I asked him about finding the MP.

'He's around somewhere, let me introduce you. I rather liked him.'

After a lot of looking around, helped by Peter's six-foot plus height, we saw Mr. Roberts MP talking to a small group of young men in grey suits, and elbowed our way towards him. By the way his face relaxed when he saw Peter, I got the feeling that the liking had been mutual.

We were introduced and after vainly attempting to have a conversation and failing against the background noise, decided to leave the reception and go to the members' bar in the hope that it would be quiet enough to hear each other speak. I could see why Peter liked Mr. Roberts. Underneath the savvy politician and businessman was a kind and vulnerable person. A handsome woman looked into the members' room and smiled and waved at him .

'Allow me to introduce you to my wife, Janet.' He put his arm around her shoulders and gave her a gentle hug. It looked like a happy marriage to my inexperienced eyes. Mr.

Roberts and Peter were having an animated conversation about sailing. I overheard an invitation being offered to Peter and his delighted acceptance. Janet, meanwhile, had taken my arm and suggested that we leave them to it and find a seat, a drink and have a chat. How could I refuse?

'Thank you, Chas, for your help in finding my husband.' I made the usual and expected responses and waited for her to open up the discussion. Being a mediator has its uses. I knew that so far we were only seeing the tip of the iceberg.

'I usually let my husband and son get on with their own lives, I'm too busy to pay them too much attention.'

I said nothing and waited for her to continue. She sat very still and looked at her husband before turning to me.

'They are both in a difficult position and I can't work out how best to help. Although he is my son, unfortunately Jim is not a good businessman. He makes promises he can't keep and has been a lot of trouble to us. We have bailed him out more times than I care to think about. We have usually had to find some money, but this time it's more serious, he could have been taken to court. The only way to stop it was for my husband to stay away from the planning meeting. So the plans were agreed, in the absence of any serious opposition. My husband was put in a no-win situation. By protecting Jim he upset me, and more importantly, he has upset his constituents, who were relying on him to oppose the development. This might mean the end of his political career.'

I made some sympathetic noises. She went on, 'He has also upset RD Ventures, who were not too keen on the development. However, they are part of the development consortium so will have to go along with the decision.'

I was getting confused. Even a bright spark like me sometimes loses the plot.

'So why were RD Ventures against the development?'

'The sister of the CEO is the headmistress of the school, which will be affected if the development goes ahead.' I remembered that Ella had told me that Alexander was CEO of RD Ventures. Some of the issues raised by the mediation were beginning to make more sense.

'Maybe you need a mediator,' I said with a smile, which I hoped showed that I wasn't really serious.

'We may well need something; I don't know what. I just wish Jim would grow up. He seems to think he can rely on charm to get him anywhere. He has to learn that it has its limits.'

I thought about Ella and wished that she could hear this conversation.

CHAPTER 12
ELLA

I had a rather fraught chat with Chas yesterday, with the result that I didn't sleep well last night. He was very critical of Jim. Apparently even his mother is getting fed up with his goings-on. I need to talk to him, Jim that is.

So I phoned Jim and we agreed to meet for a drink after he leaves his office. I got butterflies thinking about it and rushed out and bought a new sweater to wear. It is a soft lavender colour and cashmere. An extravagance but I hope it will be worth it. I thought I would use the Chas approach and arrive a little late. Despite that, I arrived at the wine bar before Jim. He's even worse than Chas for punctuality. My parents wouldn't approve. They are dead keen on being on time.

As usual Jim looked gorgeous. He gave me a peck on the cheek and ordered a bottle of Pouilly-Fumé; I like it a lot but don't buy it myself because it's too expensive.

'I'm so pleased that your father is OK, I could see how upset you were about his disappearing.'

'I suppose it was my entire fault really.'

'How come?'

'He was looking after me again. I had got myself into a business problem and by missing the planning meeting he got me out of it.'

I didn't say anything and just leaned towards him and touched his arm.

'He's rescued me before but this time it upset my mother. She is very proud of my father, especially his political career, and she thinks this may be damaging to it.'

Jim looked chastened in a wolf-like way. I could see that he wanted to howl but wouldn't. I admired his self-control and stroked his arm some more.

'Your parents sound like very good people,' I said.

'They are, too good to me. I don't deserve their support. I know that I have been a worry and a disappointment. I started off so well then it all seemed to go wrong.'

'What happened?'

'A trivial thing, really. When I was a student, I had a girlfriend who I planned to marry. Then she met Alexander at a party, and it was all over between us. She was bowled over by him for a while and dumped me. It didn't lead to anything but even when it was over between them, she didn't want to come back to me. She said that now she'd seen what it was like being with a clever fascinating man she knew that she could never be happy with me.'

'How awful for you, Jim. That was a long time ago. You've had women since then. Julia, for instance, is beautiful.'

'I know, but for some reason it had a bad effect on me, on my confidence perhaps. I feel as if I've been running to catch up ever since.'

I didn't tell Jim, but Chas has a theory that we spend most of our lives defending and trying to improve our self-esteem. I think that Jim's story would back up his theory.

We drank the wine and another couple of glasses. I put a lot of energy into charming Jim. I was sympathetic, flattering, flirting and gradually his mood improved, and he even flirted back. I had a sense that this was my chance to get closer to him.

'Let's go back to my place for a whisky or a coffee.' I held my breath and crossed my fingers while I waited for his answer.

'Thank you, Ella, that sounds like a nice idea.'

Phew, I said to myself.

I am a tidy person so I knew that my flat would be welcoming. I had even changed the sheets on my bed, just in case.

The first move into a possible sexual adventure is for me an exciting risk because of the possibility of rejection. I had prepared the ground, but was it enough? We had both drunk rather a lot so that we could use that as an excuse for whatever happened. I can't say for sure who made the sexual step inevitable, but I am prepared to take the responsibility. After all, I had thought about it long and often enough. My bed looked inviting. I had used my best cotton sheets. The lighting was excellent, flattering and warm and cosy. We undressed down to our underwear, my most sexy, recently acquired. As I had predicted, Jim looked like a model for underpants in his. So far, so good.

Alcohol may be beneficial in lowering inhibitions, but it doesn't do much for other physiological functions. At least I hope that was the reason for our inability to do more than just fumble around and eventually slip into sleep.

The next morning neither of us said a word about it. Jim got up and rushed off. I sat in my kitchen drinking coffee and going over the previous evening. For reasons which I didn't understand, I felt an even stronger attachment to Jim.

CHAPTER 13
PETER

Two days after the reception at the Royal Academy I had a phone call from Roger Roberts. It had been a pleasure to see him. To my surprise he asked me if I would like to go on a weekend sailing trip with him. I told him that I would like that very much and he said that he would call me to suggest some dates. So when he called, I expected that it would be to set up a sailing weekend. The man is full of surprises. He asked if I would go with him on a business trip.

'I would appreciate your help and support, Peter. It would be work for you, so I am happy to pay your usual fees and expenses.'

I like him, and since I don't have much on at the moment I agreed.

All he told me was that the meeting was in Bridport in Dorset, and we agreed that he would pick me up at eight o'clock the following Monday.

'It's not the best place to get to by public transport so I'll drive. It should take us about three hours if we are lucky. I'll tell you more on the journey.'

I was intrigued.

Roger was punctual and we set off just after eight o'clock. Since we were driving out of London the traffic was light and we made good progress. Roger was a good driver in a powerful car, so by mid-morning we had left the motorways and were driving much more sedately on smaller roads in

Dorset. It is one of my favourite counties. The shapes of the hills look prehistoric and from time to time we saw glimpses of the sea. We stopped for a coffee break in Dorchester. Roger hadn't said much during the drive.

'I don't talk much when I drive,' he said. 'I like to focus on the driving.'

Over coffee, he told me the agenda for the day. He had been offered a consultancy by the development consortium and their offices were in Bridport. I didn't pass any comment although my thoughts went to the issue of the revolving door.

I think he must have noticed my reaction because he started to explain his position.

'I know that I am taking a bit of a risk, but if you don't take chances, you might as well not be alive. Some of my constituents think that I have let them down so I may not survive the next general election. This could be my fallback position.'

He looked at me and I felt that he was hoping that I wouldn't disapprove. I suppose I did, really, but chose not to reveal that to him as he seemed too vulnerable. Who am I to judge?

We arrived at Bridport well before lunchtime. Roger's meeting was at 2 pm so we decided to have lunch in a charming old hotel in the High Street. It wasn't busy. The offices were in a Georgian town house just around the corner in the next street. I had a pint of local beer and Roger had a glass of sparkling water.

'I need to be wide awake for this meeting,' he explained.

The front door of the offices was black and very shiny and the whole house looked in immaculate condition. I suppose that if you are in the construction business, you can at least look after your own property. We were shown into a spacious waiting room on the first floor and offered coffee. Just after two o'clock, we were taken to a large office at the front of the building that looked out onto the street. Roger had told the person who set up the meeting that I was his secretary and he wanted me to be in on the meeting and any subsequent discussions.

The furniture did justice to the lovely old building and must have cost lots of money. A short fat man held out his hand to Roger and introduced himself as Dr. David Fish, chairman of the consortium of developers, one of whom was RD Ventures. Two other directors of the consortium sat round an oval mahogany board table. David Fish invited us to join them and made the introductions. I noticed that Roger seemed reluctant to make eye contact with anyone.

'Thank you for agreeing to meet us, Mr. Roberts. I hope for a discussion from which we can all benefit.'

Roger nodded, although his face looked sad.

'We are aware of your interest and experience in planning. I understand that you have been involved in the processes for obtaining planning permissions in your constituency for some years.'

'You're correct. I have considerable experience in planning issues. Before I became an MP I worked as an architect in a large London practice. I have always been interested in the built environment and how it can improve lives.'

David Fish looked down at the papers in front of him.

'We need a consultant to help us deal with planning matters, someone who has a good grasp of the pitfalls and how to circumvent them.'

'As you know, I am currently an MP, so it would not be possible at this point in time for me to play that role.'

'Why is that?'

'Two reasons. There may be a conflict of interest between my job as an MP and being a consultant for you.'

'And the other reason?'

'Being an MP is a full-time job, so I just won't have the time to give you.'

David Fish looked at the other directors, who both gave him a slight nod of the head.

'I understand,' he said, 'so I have a suggestion to make.'

Roger looked apprehensive and gently rubbed his eyebrow.

'For the time being, we could just ask your advice from time to time. There would be no formal agreement between us, for the moment; it would all be very low-key. Then at some point in the future, if you change your mind and have more time, we could set up the consultancy on a more formal basis.'

Roger gave a gentle sigh, of relief, I assumed. There was a bit more general discussion on matters around the construction industry. Then David Fish thanked us for driving down and hoped that we would have a good return journey.

Roger drove fast and said little. I allowed my thoughts to wander about where this vague deal might lead. I said nothing but promised myself that I would follow events as far as I could with interest and concern.

When we arrived at my place, I invited him in for a drink, not really expecting him to accept.

'Thank you, Peter, I'd welcome that.'

We settled down in my rather small sitting room, with glasses of whisky.

'I'm in a bit of a difficult position with the consortium,' he said. 'I did a favour once for David Fish, a few years ago. It was a bad decision on my part.'

I sipped my whisky and looked at him in what I hoped was a friendly and encouraging way.

'I put a government contract his way. I made sure that there was no open tendering process, so he had no competition. Bad form. Against parliamentary rules and so on.'

I just nodded.

'It happens,' I said.

'I can't blame Jim. It was while he was still at university.'

'So why did you?' I asked.

'I think I was on an ego trip. I'd just become an MP, it must have gone to my head. I thought I could do anything. The money was too tempting to resist, so I didn't. Perhaps that's why I've covered up for Jim all this time. He probably gets it from me.'

'I can see that it makes it difficult to deal with David Fish and the consortium now,' I said.

'Yes, I could be exposed and that would be the end of my political career.'

I didn't have any answers. So we just sat sipping our drinks until he decided that it was time to leave.

CHAPTER 14
CHAS

Ella isn't a bad-looking woman, but when I saw her at our last mediation, she looked pale and wan, I think is the best way to describe it. It was a complex case and went on until early evening, leaving Ella struggling a bit. As usual at the close of a mediation we finish the paperwork together and have a bit of a debrief. Ella looked just about done in by the time we had finished so I asked her if she would like a drink. There is a wine bar on the way to the Tube station so we agreed to have a drink before going home.

Ella has the potential to be an excellent mediator but today she hadn't been at her best. She had seemed distracted and didn't pay attention at her usual level. I gave her a few openings to tell me what the matter was while we were having our bottle of wine. She didn't respond and seemed flat and distant. She is usually good company, but it was as if her attention was somewhere else. Probably with Jim. We neither of us wanted to prolong the evening and left after about an hour together.

I got back to my house in Chelsea and decided to spend a quiet evening at home. That is no hardship; it's a lovely house and feels especially cosy on a winter evening. I downloaded some Bernstein, poured myself a dry sherry and sat in my favourite armchair with my feet up on a footstool. As usual I went over the mediation, thinking about how we could have reached a resolution. This one had resulted in a sort of stalemate. Despite hours of discussion and negotiation each party had stuck to their guns. The next time they met would be in court, at great expense to all concerned. When mediations fail to get an agreement, I spend time analysing what prevented it and working out what, if anything, we could have done to change the outcome. There is no point in blaming anyone; we just need to learn from it. Ella had been in a strange mood all day. She is usually on top of the case and has useful insights. Today she was, not to put too fine a point on it, a dead loss. I needed to find out what was happening because she was no use as a mediator in her present state.

Despite my worries, after a couple of glasses of sherry and the stirring music from *West Side Story* I felt pleased when my phone rang. I recognised the lovely velvety voice of Julia and my evening took a turn for the better. To my surprise she said that she wanted to ask my advice and offered to take me out to dinner. Naturally I agreed and we fixed a date for the following evening. There seemed to be some urgency about the meeting.

When I put the phone down, I poured myself another drink and settled in to thinking about the dinner invitation and its possible agenda. I expect that it's about Jim; he seems to take up a lot of a lot of people's time.

Julia had suggested that we meet at a new restaurant in Spitalfields. I got there a few minutes late and Julia was waiting in the entrance of the converted warehouse.

'Hello Chas, good of you to come. We can't stay here, it's far too noisy, and we won't be able to have a proper discussion. Do you mind if we go to my flat? It's only a short taxi ride.'

It certainly was impossible to have a quiet conversation at the restaurant, so I agreed, despite wondering what we were going to have to eat. I was hungry and looking forward to dinner and a bottle of wine. When we arrived at her flat in St. John's Wood it was soon clear that I had worried for nothing. She immediately poured a glass of chilled Chablis and laid the dining table with poached salmon, and my favourite rye bread. While I was sipping the wine, she quickly put together a colourful salad.

'Let's just eat and talk later, Chas.'

'Good idea,' I said.

We sat at the table, eating and making small talk. After some French cheese and fruit we moved from the table and took our glasses and another bottle of wine and sat on two matching blue velvet sofas at the other end of the large open-plan room. By the look of it, Julia was doing well. Both flat and furnishing were at the high end of the market. I was beginning to wonder when we were going to get onto the agenda for the meeting but decided to let Julia set the pace. We were well into our second bottle of wine when she said, 'I want to talk to you about Jim and Ella.'

She told me that she had met Jim though his father. He had been looking for a lawyer to take care of Jim's business affairs and she had been recommended. They had met and got on well and she had been Jim's lawyer ever since.

'We have been though quite a lot together. As you know, Jim can be difficult at times. I was struggling to get started in my career until I worked for Jim; now, as you can see, I'm doing very well. I don't want to lose what I've worked so hard to get.'

She paused, looking closely at me as if measuring my response so far. I am a mediator, so I don't give much away unless I want to. I just nodded, encouraging her to carry on.

'I'm now very closely tied up with Jim in all sorts of ways.' I looked questioningly at her, so she continued, 'I have been taken into the family. I don't have a family of my own so it's good to part of the Roberts' family. Jim and I are lovers and I see my future with him. I am worried about what is going on between him and Ella. Something is, I'm sure of that.'

'Ella doesn't tell me about her personal life. We are colleagues but she doesn't confide in me. I am rather concerned about Ella, as it happens. She is not her usual self, preoccupied a lot of the time.'

'I get the sense that she listens to you.'

'I suppose she does sometimes. I know she wants to be a good mediator and she knows that I will support her in this goal.'

'It will not be good for her if she pursues her relationship with Jim.'

'Isn't that up to her and Jim?' I said, although I agreed with her.

'If you want the best for Ella, try and persuade her to back off.'

'She's very much her own person, so I don't think that she would respond positively to being told what to do.'

'Believe me, Chas, I'm not just being a jealous lover. There's a lot she doesn't know or understand. She should get out while she can.'

I looked at Julia and raised my eyebrows.

'Let's change the subject. How about another glass of wine?'

I accepted and we sat and talked for another hour or so. Now the main purpose of the evening had been dealt with we discussed what exhibitions and events we had been to recently. We discovered that we both liked American composers and floated the idea that we might go to a concert together. It was after ten when I called a taxi. Julia thanked me for listening and gave me a kiss on the cheek when I left. During my taxi ride home, I thought about what Julia had said and I had the feeling that it was just the tip of another iceberg.

CHAPTER 15
CHAS

Two days after my dinner and conversation with Julia I had a phone call from Alexander Farr. I hadn't seen or heard from him since the mediation. He had paid his bill promptly and filled in an evaluation form about the mediation. He had been very positive in his comments, despite the fact that he had paid rather a lot of money to Jim. He seemed to think that it had been worth it. He asked if we could meet for a drink and a chat. Remembering the noise level in the restaurant where I had met with Julia a few days ago, I asked if he would be prepared to come to my house. When I explained the reason for my suggestion he readily agreed.

I do enjoy inviting people to my house. It has a good atmosphere. I've lived in it for years and can't ever imagine leaving. I don't go for all this modern white furniture so my house is filled with old dark furniture, some of which belonged to my parents. They worked in Africa and India and my house contains stuff from their stints abroad. I suppose it's rather like an old-fashioned gentlemen's club.

He arrived on time, and we went to my first-floor sitting room. I poured him a gin and tonic and me a dry sherry. I made a few remarks about the state of the economy and then waited quietly for him to begin. He said nothing for a while, and we sipped our drinks in silence. It was a good silence and gave me the chance to really look at him. He was formally dressed in a dark suit and white shirt. His short dark hair shone, he looked fit and strong although he was small and compact. I expected that the conversation would be about Jim; he seemed to be causing a lot of disturbance. So I was surprised when he said that he wanted to talk about Roger Roberts, Jim's dad.

'I want to ask your advice about a decision made by my partners in the building consortium that my company RD Ventures is a part of. They want to employ Roger Roberts MP as a planning consultant. I don't think it's a good idea.'

'Is he allowed to do that while he's an MP?'

'Lots of MPs work as consultants. I don't agree with it, but it goes on.'

'Why are you against it, do you know him?'

'I have never met him but he's not the problem. It's because he is Jim's dad and, as I have found to my cost, Jim can mean trouble. He has gone out on a limb already to rescue Jim, so as far as I am concerned, because Jim is a liability, then so is he.'

'Yes, I can see what you are getting at. I don't really see how I can help.'

'I am going to have to go against my partners on this, which is difficult since they have already talked to Mr. Roberts.'

'Have they offered him a consultancy?'

'Yes, but so far, he hasn't accepted. He says that he doesn't have the time at the moment.'

'So what's the problem?'

'This isn't going to go away. They have enough on Jim to be able to have considerable influence on his father and they will want to take advantage of that, if not immediately, then at some time soon.'

'The penny is beginning to drop. I still don't see how I can help.'

'I'm not clear myself, at the moment. It is good to be able to discuss it with someone who can think clearly. Your mediation skills might be useful.'

I was surprised at the pleasure it gave me to have Alexander show his appreciation. I stood up.

'How do you fancy a sandwich and a glass of wine? I feel a bit hungry, and we can continue our discussion in the kitchen.'

Alexander smiled. 'Great idea, I already feel better now that I've got that off my chest.'

We went downstairs to my kitchen, which is at the back of the house overlooking a small patio garden. It was dark so I closed the blinds. Unlike the rest of my house, the kitchen is all slate grey and stainless-steel modernity. I made us some cold beef sandwiches and offered beer or wine. We opened a bottle of Rioja and sat down at the breakfast bar. It felt natural, as if we had been friends for years.

'Let's not talk about my problems anymore, I want to hear about you. How did you get into mediation?'

I am usually a reserved person but with Alexander I felt free enough to tell him about my journey from becoming a barrister to choosing mediation. He seemed genuinely interested. We didn't want to stop talking, so when we had drunk the bottle of wine, we decided to open another.

'I gather you live here alone.' I nodded.

'Are you happy with that?'

No-one had ever asked me that before, so I was unprepared and didn't know how to answer. I felt my acquired sophistication melt away as the evening slipped into night. Nothing was said but I felt the atmosphere change between us. We looked at each other in surprise.

'I suppose it's time to call a cab, it's nearly midnight.' I hid my disappointment.

'Can we meet again?' said Alexander, to my profound relief.

We shook hands when he left, and we both knew that something important had just begun.

CHAPTER 16
PETER

As promised, Roger Roberts invited me to spend a day sailing with him. On a Tuesday morning we made an early start and he drove us down to the yacht marina in Lymington. During the journey we didn't talk much. He is a fast driver and I thought it prudent to let him focus on that. The weather was excellent for a sail down the Solent towards Cowes. We carried out the pre-sail tasks, let the engine warm up and slipped skillfully out of the mooring and motored into the river. Roger didn't say much other than to give me instructions; he was clearly a competent sailor. We passed the Isle of Wight ferry as it entered the river and waved at the few people standing on the upper decks. After passing the distinctive markings for the entrance to the Lymington River, Roger turned the yacht into the wind, and I raised the mainsail. We headed down the Solent and I pulled out the jib. It was a pleasant force four on our beam and we made good speed towards Cowes.

At about eleven o'clock Roger went below to make us a coffee and I took the helm. I enjoyed the feel of the boat moving, the chuckle of the water and the sight of the wind filling the sails. There were only a few other boats. I felt as if we had the Solent all to ourselves, well almost. As we got nearer to Cowes, I could see that on the shore were a few enormous houses. I pointed one out to Roger when we were sipping his excellent coffee.

'It's even more impressive close up,' said Roger. I looked surprised.

'Do you know who owns it?'

'No, but I went there for a meeting with a group of people from the development consortium.'

'The people we met in Bridport?'

'Yes. They seem to have access to several such places. So far, we haven't been to any place more than once. Heaven only knows who owns them.'

I thought about the implications of what Roger had just said and decided to keep my questions until later. We were nearing the entrance to Cowes and there was suddenly a lot to do, sails to get down, fenders to get out and put in place. We concentrated on what was necessary and eventually Roger nudged us into a berth in the marina.

We were both more than ready for lunch. Roger suggested a local pub which served simple food in large portions. After we had each had a pint of beer and had ordered our pies and chips, I told Roger how much I had enjoyed the sail.

'I need it, especially at the moment. I don't think about anything else except the sailing when I am on my boat.'

'How are things, Roger?' I ventured to ask. I was torn between concern and wanting to know and not wishing to spoil his day.

'It would be helpful to chat to you about things, but I would prefer to wait until we got back. I've brought some pasta and sauce that we can have for dinner on the boat, if that's all right with you.'

'Sounds fine,' I said, and we changed the conversation to share sailing experiences. We didn't stay long in the pub.

We needed to get going on the return tide so after an hour or so we took a stroll around Cowes and then returned to the boat. As is the case, more often than not, we had to sail against the wind on the return passage. It took more effort and concentration but we both enjoyed the trip. Roger was the happiest I had ever seen him.

We got back into our berth at Lymington about six o'clock. Together we efficiently tidied the mainsail and 'put the boat to bed' as Roger put it. Then we opened a bottle of Beaujolais which I had brought with me, and Roger cooked our dinner. We sat below in the cosy cabin. I had decided to wait for Roger to raise any issues that he wanted to discuss, and I didn't have to wait for long.

'You know, Peter, awarding planning permission is like a Faustian pact.'

'What do you mean exactly?' I asked.

'Well, the developers in the early stages offer all sorts of sweeteners, such as a traffic calming scheme or affordable housing, so that their plans are accepted. Then they use so-called viability studies to show that they can't offer as many affordable houses as they first said because this would prevent them from making a certain level of profit. Much of this is hidden because of commercial confidentiality.'

'Can't say that I'm surprised. Is this an issue for you?'

'Well, you remember that meeting in Bridport?' I nodded. 'Since then, I have been requested to attend several meetings.'

'But you told them that you weren't able to be a consultant while you were still an MP.'

'Perhaps requested is the wrong word to use. The right one is ordered.'

'Can't you refuse?'

'No, because Jim has behaved foolishly again. I can't take the risk.'

'What is the risk?'

'That Jim would be prosecuted for not fulfilling contracts. I can't take that risk. He has got himself into a great deal of debt. A prosecution would be the end for him.'

The benefit of the day's sailing hadn't lasted long. Roger's face was now drawn so that he looked a much older man. I felt lost for words. Roger was putting his own career at risk for his son. I sensed that he was a good kind man who couldn't see a way out of this predicament. The family loyalty was too strong.

'Is there anything I can do to help?'

'It's good to be able to talk about it. I can't tell my wife, she would be too upset. She knows a lot about Jim and his weaknesses, but his latest cock-up might be the last straw for her.'

'What is the development consortium asking you to do?'

'They aren't making much progress with the local authority with their latest submission, so they want me to help them with their negotiations. They already have several high-powered lawyers on board who can run rings around most local authorities, but apparently this time they have come up against some hard resistance. That is why they are leaning on me.'

'So what's your plan?'

'I'm just treading water at the moment. I've said that I will look at what has happened to date and then come up with some suggestions for the best way to proceed.'

'Sounds a good plan.'

Roger sighed.

'Let's pack up and get back. Thank you for listening to me, it does help.'

'Remember what I said. If I can help, let me know. I still have some useful friends from my military days.'

On the drive back to London we talked about other matters. When Roger dropped me at my place, he shook my hand and thanked me for a good day. As he drove away, I thought to myself that families were a mixed blessing.

CHAPTER 17
ELLA

I have had several missed phone calls from Chas; he seems keen to meet up for some reason. For reasons of my own I have been avoiding him; it's not him I want to see on my phone display, it's Jim. I don't feel able to walk away from him. In fact, I have been fighting the temptation to call him. It's just as well there are no mediations in the pipeline at the moment. I can't get my mind around anything; it's too full of Jim.

My best friend invited me to spend the day with her. We do this from time to time. A walk by the river, lunch in a pub, then a couple of glasses of wine and dinner at her place. I usually stay the night so that we don't have to worry about the drinking. We talk about all sorts of stuff. At first I hesitated to tell her about Jim, but she knows me so well that she guessed that something was up. She is a good listener, so I ended up telling her about him. Over the years we have been friends, we must have spent hours talking about men, but we never seem to reach a resolution. We laugh about it. Maybe if we thought more about ourselves, we might be in more powerful places.

'Don't put all your eggs in one basket,' was her advice. 'Get on with your own goals in life and don't make him the focal point.'

When you feel like I do now that's easier said than done. I have been there for her when she has had some very bad times with men. I think she was pleased to be able to be there for me.

*

The next day, Jim called. We made the usual bland polite remarks, then to my amazement and delight he said, 'Are you free on the weekend?'

When I said that I was he asked me if I fancied a weekend in Lyme Regis. Apparently, a friend of his has a cottage there which he was happy to rent to Jim. My day suddenly went from grey to gold.

'What a lovely idea, I would really like that,' I said, trying not to sound too excited although I could feel my heart beating faster. We briefly discussed the arrangement. He would drive us down on Friday afternoon. I offered to provide some food for breakfast and dinner.

'Good plan. Don't worry about Saturday, we'll find somewhere to dine out.'

I am always surprised when reminded that a phone call can either make or ruin the day. When I put the phone down, I jumped up and down with excitement. Two days to get ready. I knew that I would enjoy every minute of deciding what to wear and what clothes to take. Even providing the food would be a source of pleasure as I planned and prepared a meal for Friday night when we arrived. I imagined that we would spend the days walking the coastal path, having pub lunches then having sexy relaxing evenings. I hoped the cottage had a log fire and decided to take some candles to improve the evening ambience.

The time passed quickly, and Jim picked me up as we had agreed. For some reason I expected him to turn up in an SUV. That seemed to match his role in life. I was wrong. He drove up in a sporty white BMW. Friday afternoon is not the best time to be driving out of London, so it took some time to get onto the motorway. Once we were, we made good time and were driving down the steep hill into Lyme Regis just as it was getting dark. The cottage was on the East Cliff, just a short distance out of town. There was a small garage, outside which we parked the car. Jim got out and retrieved the key to the cottage from under the large stone. He opened the door and went inside to turn on some lights.

The living room, kitchen and dining room were all on the first floor. Although it was dark, I could see that there were sea views from windows to the front and side. The cottage had two bedrooms, one on the ground floor and one on the first floor with sea views. We looked at one another and smiled. It was a great place. There was a wood-burning stove and Jim got that going while I prepared our dinner. I was glad that I had brought the candles. All in all, it was a romantic atmosphere. I cringed at myself for being so conventional. Jim liked it and was friendly and affectionate. We didn't stay up late. In our first-floor bedroom the window looked out to sea. We left the curtains open so we would wake up to the sound and the sight of the waves. On my happiness meter I reached the top of the scale. I had fancied Jim ever since I first set eyes on him at the mediation. The feelings were getting stronger. I didn't want to be anywhere else or with anybody else, this was where I belonged. I couldn't sleep; I didn't want to waste a second, so I snuggled up to Jim who was snoring gently.

I must have slept eventually because the next thing I knew was the sound of activity in the kitchen. I sat up in bed. The light streamed in, a pale grey light which gradually turned to light blue then to a deep turquoise. It was going to be a lovely autumn day.

The coffee smelt strong, so I called to Jim to ask him to add plenty of milk. He brought it into our bedroom. What a wonderful way to start the day. Jim looked gorgeous; he was, to my slight disappointment, already dressed. His clothes suggested a walking agenda. I didn't really mind what we did so long as we did it together. So I dressed in my walking gear and went down to prepare breakfast.

I got out the bacon and eggs from the refrigerator.

'I don't want much breakfast, just some toast. I'll make some more coffee.' I felt a bit deflated. I was getting used to his moodiness. It's amazing what you put up with when you are in this early stage of a relationship. So I just smiled, and put the bacon and eggs back in the refrigerator.

'I'm looking forward to a walk,' I said, trying to lift the mood.

'Good, we can do a coastal walk this morning and have a pub lunch.'

Jim had brought a walking map and we drove to the pub car park which was to be the starting point of the walk. It was a lovely day and it seemed to have a positive effect on Jim. I've always been a bit of a twitcher; I like to watch birds, especially their behaviour. I could see some turnstones, beautiful small birds who were turning over stones at the water's edge, looking for food underneath them. I felt like them, turning things over, wondering what was underneath.

I pointed them out to Jim, and it brought a smile to his face. As we walked on Jim began to talk about his business plans. They sounded like wishful thinking to me. I wanted to be supportive, so I said, 'Sounds good, Jim. How about the rest of your life, what are your plans?'

I thought that it was reckless of me to ask because I probably wouldn't like the answer.

'No plans at the moment.'

The relief I felt lifted my spirits and I decided to enjoy the rest of the walk and not ask any more questions. When we returned to the pub, we were both hungry after our light breakfast, so we ordered a hearty lunch and took our drinks to sit outside. After lunch we drove back to Lyme Regis and spent the afternoon wandering around the town and small harbour. Jim had booked a table in a restaurant for dinner. It was in walking distance from the cottage. Over dinner he returned to his plans for developing his business.

'Dad is well in with this development consortium, he should be able to put a lot of contracts my way. He is thinking of joining the company when he leaves politics.'

'Is he planning to do that soon?' I asked.

'He keeps saying that he wants to leave, and then he can't bring himself to do it. I think he likes the power and status.'

'That's understandable.'

'Yea, but money brings power and status, with fewer constraints.'

I wasn't too happy where this conversation was heading because I didn't want my warm glow towards Jim to fade anytime soon. He was too attractive.

'What shall we do tomorrow?' I asked.

Jim sipped his red wine and then put his hand on my knee under the table.

'I think we should have a late breakfast and then drive home via Bridport. We can stop there for a look around and a coffee or a light lunch.'

'Isn't it out of our way?'

'Not much. To be honest, I want to have a look at the offices of the development consortium. They are in Bridport.'

I don't know why, but I felt disturbed by this idea. I drank my wine, and the waiter came and refilled my glass. *What the hell*, I thought, *just enjoy the evening.* We walked back up the hill to the cottage. Jim had put a bottle of champagne in the refrigerator; he poured us each a glass. We sat in the candlelight and listened to the sea.

The next morning, we had our tea in bed. We were more at one in bed than anywhere else. When he made love, Jim was considerate, generous and he knew what parts of me to stroke and suck. I put the thoughts of how he knew so much out of my mind and made the most of the pleasure since a regular supply of it was not guaranteed. Eventually I recovered sufficiently to get up and cook our breakfast. By mid-morning we had packed the car, put the key back under the stone and driven away. I am not normally a sentimental person, but I did have tears in my eyes. Jim set the satnav for Bridport and didn't look back.

CHAPTER 18
CHAS

When I saw that it was Alexander calling, I could feel my heart beating faster. I had resolved that I would make contact with him after our last evening together, but he had beaten me to it. Since our last meeting I had dreamt about him and found it difficult to concentrate, my head was full of him.

'Hello, Chas, do you have a moment? I need to talk to you.'

I could tell from his voice that something was wrong.

'Of course, is everything all right?'

'No, afraid not, our offices have been burgled, the head office in Bridport. Can I come and see you?'

'Can it wait until this evening? We can talk over dinner,' I replied, remembering our last evening at my house.

'Yes, that would be excellent, is seven all right?'

I prepared a light meal, opened a bottle of Rioja, and dressed with care. Alexander always looks as if he is just about to attend an important meeting, so I endeavoured to look smart. He arrived ten minutes early, carrying a bottle of wine and his briefcase. As I took his coat, he touched my arm. We went upstairs to my sitting room. When we had settled into our armchairs with a drink, I said, 'OK, tell me what's happened.'

'I had a call this morning from the secretary in the Bridport offices. Apparently, they were broken into last night. No damage, the lock had been picked but some files have gone missing.'

'Any in particular?'

'Yes, contracts that RD Ventures and the rest of the consortium had with Jim Roberts and correspondence about his failure to deliver.'

'I thought that it was all done electronically these days.'

'You're right, most of it is. They took two computers as well. So in addition to the stuff about Jim, they also now have access to the accounts of the company, as well as future development plans.'

'Have you any idea who did this?'

'I've been thinking about it all day, as you can imagine. Perhaps it was Jim. The consortium has enough information on him to ruin his business.'

'As well as blackmailing his father,' I reminded him.

As I got up to pour us another drink, I remembered that Ella had told me that she and Jim had been to Lyme Regis for a few days and came home via Bridport. Should I mention this to Alexander? To give myself some time to work out what to do, I suggested that we went down to the kitchen so that I could finish preparing our meal. As I grilled the fish and steamed the vegetables, I tried to recall what Ella had actually said. She was so thrilled to have been with Jim that she was sparing on the details. When she is with him everything else pales into insignificance and she only sees what she wants to see. I made the decision to say nothing to Alexander until I had another chat with Ella.

'What are you doing about the burglary? Have you informed the police?'

'I thought that perhaps we should, but the others in the consortium said that they didn't want any publicity, so we agreed not to involve them. Actually, I was rather relieved. If Jim was the burglar, I don't want to be the cause of more trouble in his life.'

I nodded my understanding. During dinner we didn't mention the subject again.

'Let's talk about something else now, Chas, I feel much better just talking to you about things. Got any exciting plans at the moment?'

'No, I have had a flurry of mediations. When they come up, I feel obliged to accept them. I have a quiet few days coming up. How about you?'

'I've been working very hard and feel ready for some relaxation. Perhaps we could go to a concert? You said you like music.'

'I can't think of anything I'd like better.'

After dinner, we went back upstairs to our cosy armchairs, and I poured us each a good measure of Armagnac. Although he tried hard to hide it, I could see that Alexander was still worrying about the burglary. I let the silence hang in the hope that he would tell me what was on his mind. He said nothing. So I got up, walked over to him and put my hand on his shoulder.

'Is there anything you want to tell me?' I asked quietly.

Alexander looked up at me. 'I'm frightened, Chas, Jim is a loose cannon. What do you think he's up to?'

'We are not even certain that Jim was the burglar, we just have to wait to see what happens.'

'I have to do something. I really want to know, but without police involvement.'

'I could ask my old friend, Peter, to look into it. I don't think you've met him. He has done a few little jobs for me in the past. I trust him. He has a lot of useful contacts so he may be able to help.'

'I don't see that I have much choice.'

'I expect that you'd like to meet him, shall I arrange it?'

'Yes, I'd appreciate that.'

Alexander had finished his drink. He relaxed into the armchair and smiled.

'You are becoming a very special friend, Chas.' I didn't attempt to hide my pleasure.

'Good, I'll set up a meeting as soon as possible.'

CHAPTER 19
PETER

My old friend Chas is putting a lot of work my way. He called me to set up a meeting with a friend of his called Alexander. It's a small world. He is the CEO of RD Ventures, one of the members of the consortium who offered a job to Roger Roberts MP. We met in a room, booked by Chas, in his chambers. They do all right, these barristers. The room was wood-panelled, with high ceilings and gold-framed pictures of judges around the walls. I could feel the weight of the law all around me.

Chas and Alexander were already there, sitting at a large mahogany table drinking tea. There was a silver tray with another cup and saucer on it, for me I assumed.

Chas made the introductions, poured me a cup of tea, then said, 'Over to you, Alexander.'

'I am keen to find out who broke into the consortium's offices in Bridport. There was no damage, just the theft of paperwork and two computers, which contain information on future development plans as well as company accounts.'

'Is that everything?' I enquired, giving Alexander an encouraging smile.

'There were also copies of contracts with other companies and individuals.'

There were a few minutes' silence. I drank my tea while I decided what to say.

'I just want to tell you about my real concern,' said Alexander.

'Good, I think that would be helpful.'

'I believe that a man called Jim Roberts stole the documents and computers. I am particularly keen that he does not get into any trouble due to my company. I have already had enough of a bad effect on his life and I don't want to be the cause of any more distress.'

'What makes you think that Jim Roberts was the burglar?'

'Well, he has plenty of reason to want the contract and related documents. They are pretty damaging to his reputation. If they saw the light of day, it could trash his business as well as his reputation.'

'I can put your mind at rest there. It wasn't Jim Roberts, I am sure of that.'

Alexander looked relieved at my reassurance although I could see that he wasn't totally convinced.

'How do you know this?' he asked.

I had to make a quick decision. I have had a long and trusting friendship with Chas and if Alexander is a close friend of his then he must be OK.

'Because I know who did take the stuff and it wasn't Jim Roberts. Before you ask, I am afraid that I cannot tell you more. Just accept that your burglar was not Jim.'

'Thank you for telling me that, I am relieved. Of course, I understand that you can't tell me any more at the moment. We set up this meeting because I wanted to employ you to find out who did the burglary. So where do we go from here? I really do need to know.'

I thought of how I could best help them while not disclosing confidential client information.

'I need to make a few calls before saying any more. Is there another room I can use?'

Chas showed me to a small room just down the corridor. It contained a very tidy desk with papers in neat piles tied up with pink tapes.

'Do your best, Peter,' he said. 'Alexander is a good man.'

I got out my notebook and wrote down a few points. I wanted to be clear when I spoke to my client since I was going to ask his permission to tell Alexander what I knew. I got through to him at my first attempt and outlined the situation. He refused, as I thought he would.

'Think this through,' I said to him. 'He isn't going to let this go until he finds out who the burglar is. I believe that it is better if you allow me to tell him with some conditions. If he finds out without our help, and he will eventually, it could very easily damage your reputation. If you agree that I can negotiate with him, then in exchange for the information he has to agree to keep it to himself.'

'Let me think about it.'

'Well think fast, I can deal with it now if you agree. Nothing will be gained by any delay.' There was a few minutes' silence, during which I crossed my fingers. My client was a good man dealing with trying circumstances. I genuinely believed that this was the best way forward and wanted to help him.

'Well, if you think it's the best course of action.'

'I do,' I said firmly. To my relief, he agreed.

I rejoined Alexander and Chas who were sitting in what seemed like anxious silence. They both looked at me. I smiled.

'Don't look so worried. My client has agreed that I can tell you what happened. But there is a condition which you must agree to. You must agree to maintain confidentiality. My client is well-known and does not want publicity.'

'We don't have much choice. I want this over and done with.'

'I think that's a good decision. My client would like your agreement in writing. Chas, would you just produce something, please.'

While Chas went to his office to create the required paperwork, a fresh pot of tea was brought in, and Alexander and I topped up our cups. Alexander looked more relaxed, and we made desultory conversation while we waited. I was also working out the best way to tell Alexander about the burglary. Chas returned with papers to be signed by Alexander and witnessed by him. I cleared my throat.

'I am the burglar,' I said. Chas and Alexander looked at each other.

'My client employed me to take from the Bridport office, any material that incriminated Jim Roberts, so I took relevant paperwork and computers. The material on the computers relating to Jim Roberts has been removed and they will be returned in a few days. I was instructed to do no damage and not interfere with any other documents.'

'So who is your client?' asked Alexander.

'Since you have agreed to confidentiality, I am able to tell you that it is Roger Roberts, Jim's father. Roger spends a lot of time protecting Jim, always has done and it looks as if he always will need to. He loves Jim but that's not all. Jim's behaviour poses a potential threat to Roger's reputation and his career. The last straw has been the behaviour of some of the directors in the consortium. They are using their knowledge of Jim's wrongdoings to put pressure on Roger to work with and for them. So he asked me to carry out the burglary. I work for myself these days and make a judgment on what jobs I accept and on which clients to work for. I have spent a bit of time with Roger. He is an excellent MP, and I don't like the idea of him being ruined just because he loves his son who happens to have not turned out well.' I stopped and looked to see their reaction.

'Thank you for that, Peter. Good for you,' said Alexander. 'I will do what I can to stop the consortium bothering Roger. I begin to see why they didn't want to involve the police. Jim seems to cause problems wherever he goes, yet we all rush to protect him, including me.'

'That may not be a good strategy in the long term,' I said.

'You're probably right,' said Chas. 'Thank you Peter, it's good to have you as a friend.'

'I could do with a drink,' said Alexander. 'Anyone care to join me?'

'Love to,' said Chas. 'How about you, Peter?'

I thanked them and declined, suspecting that Roger would like to know what had happened. They shook my hand and set off together. Alexander put his arm around Chas, who smiled at him. I phoned Roger and arranged to go and see him immediately.

CHAPTER 20
ELLA

Since our trip to Lyme Regis, I haven't seen Jim. I've phoned him a few times, but he never seems to be in his office. I don't have a mobile number for him, so I just have to wait patiently, if I can, until he contacts me. I thought it had worked well when we were together, so I'm disappointed. Being cool with me is one of his distinctive features and it just makes me more eager to be with him.

When he eventually phoned, I was over the moon, as they say. We agreed to meet for dinner; he said he would organise something and pick me up early evening. As always when I meet him, I made a huge effort to look my best. He just looks great, seemingly without effort, but I know that I have to try hard. Even so, I never manage to achieve the glossy elegance that Julia has, again seemingly without effort.

He arrived on time.

'You look good, Ella. I've booked us into a restaurant overlooking the river in Maidenhead. It has a few rooms for guests, so I thought we could have a relaxing evening, stay the night, and drive back to town tomorrow. Is that all right with you?'

It was more than all right, it was wonderful. But I just said, 'What a nice idea, Jim. Thank you.'

We didn't talk much on our drive to the restaurant. Fine by me, I just enjoyed being in his car with him driving.

We sat drinking a gin and tonic in a conservatory overlooking the river.

'How long have you been working with Chas? He seems a good chap.'

I am always pleased to talk about my mediation work, so I explained that Chas was a sort of mentor helping me to get more experience and be the lead mediator with his low-key, but essential, support.

'Is he married?' asked Jim.

'No. As far as I know he's never been married.'

'Strange, he's attractive and well-off. Surprising somebody hasn't snapped him up.'

I just smiled. It wasn't up to me to tell him that Chas preferred men.

'Is he gay?' he said.

'You should ask him. We are colleagues, I don't know much about his personal life.'

'From what I hear, he has been meeting up with Alexander. What's that all about?'

'I really don't know, Jim.'

During dinner, we talked about other things. I tried to find out whether we had any interests in common. As far as I could tell, Jim didn't have any interests. In fact, he seemed dismissive of any of my suggestions, such as music or art galleries. He did admit to enjoying reading, so we did have that in common, although our tastes were rather different. He liked spy stories, especially if they were sort of true. For a moment or two, I began to look at him in a new light. During the meal we drank a bottle of wine and in the lounge afterwards, with our coffee, we both drank a couple of whiskies. I was feeling rather mellow when he said, 'Could you do something for me, Ella?'

'Yes, of course, if I can,' I replied, pleased that I could be useful to him. It could make him feel closer to me.

'I'd like to know what's going on between Alexander and Chas.'

'What do you mean?' I asked.

'Well, are they just friends, or is there some business connection?'

'Chas is a barrister and a mediator. He doesn't do business.'

'Lots of barristers are involved in business. I just wondered whether he is doing some legal work for Alexander.'

'Next time I see Chas, I'll ask him.'

'Don't tell him about our conversation, Ella.'

'Of course not, I wouldn't dream of it.'

*

In the middle of the night, I woke up, probably due to too much alcohol. I just lay in bed quietly, next to Jim, who was sort of snoring. Going over the evening conversations, I began to feel uneasy. I had no intention of questioning Chas. I already knew that he had been seeing Alexander, and that they were developing a warm friendship. What I didn't understand was why Jim was so interested in everything about Alexander. I felt that I was just seeing the tip of the iceberg again and wondered what lurked beneath.

Over breakfast I asked Jim about his ongoing business plans.

'Nothing much going on at the moment,' he said. 'I was

thinking that I might just take off for a while. Dad has an election coming up and he won't want me around. Julia has a villa in Spain. She said that I could go there anytime I wanted. I might just take up her offer.'

'Sounds lovely,' I said as my heart sank.

'I'd like to know what you discover about Alexander and Chas. How about we go out to dinner next week? We can talk about it then.'

I smiled and nodded my head, although I felt disappointment at his fixation on Alexander. After breakfast, we set off back to London. The event was overshadowed by my gradual understanding that Jim had a problem with Alexander and that he was up to something, with my connivance.

CHAPTER 21
ELLA

The week started slowly but got busier as it went on. Chas got in touch to invite me to work on a mediation with him. When I heard his voice, I knew that I couldn't spy on him, not even for Jim. What his relationship with Alexander was all about was none of my business and I decided that I would not discuss him any further with Jim.

Then, to my surprise, my next phone call was from Julia, Jim's lawyer girlfriend.

'Can we meet for lunch, Ella? There's something I wanted to discuss with you.'

Despite my small misgivings about Jim, I agreed, and we arranged to meet the next day in a pub. She suggested a pub near where I live, so I thought that she must be pretty keen to meet up. She always looks amazing, or at least she has on the few times I've seen her, so that it's quite daunting to know what to wear. I told myself not to be ridiculous, because she didn't want to meet me to discuss fashion and clothes. She had enough confidence and style of her own. Since we are not exactly friends, I dressed as if I was going to a mediation meeting, smart and businesslike.

I got to the pub first, since it was only just down the road, settled on a table and ordered a glass of sparkling water. For some reason, I felt a bit wary of seeing her. Perhaps I had a bit of a guilty conscience about spending time with Jim. When she arrived, the men in the pub looked up from whatever they were doing. The perfume arrived first, the musky type, not too strong, just enough to be noticed. She looked lovely, casually dressed in tight white trousers and a bright green jacket which showed up her unusual colouring. She looked even more striking than I remembered, and I felt drab and boring in comparison. She looked around and I waved, so she could see where I was sitting, waiting for her. As soon as she sat down a young waiter arrived to take her order, a glass of champagne. I didn't even know that the pub had champagne. We smiled at each other and made the usual small talk while we looked at the menu and ordered our lunch. When the waiter had gone away with the order, she took out her phone and showed me a picture of Jim and me in his car. It was when he had picked me up to drive down to Maidenhead.

'Did you have a nice time?' she asked. Her voice had changed, it was hard and cold.

'Yes, thank you. We went out to dinner. It was very pleasant.'

'You came back the next day, I believe.'

I didn't reply, she clearly already knew the answer. To my surprise, her eyes began to fill with tears.

'You know that Jim and I are sort of engaged, so what do you think you are doing with him?'

I swallowed; I didn't really know what to say.

'He's only using you. He hates Alexander, anything he can do to hurt him, he will. Do you know that?'

I realised that deep down, I probably did know that and hadn't wanted to acknowledge it.

'We're friends,' I said. 'It's up to Jim who he sees and how he spends his time.'

By now our lunch had arrived and I could see that neither of us had much of an appetite. We picked at the food in silence.

'We can't talk here, let's go for a walk outside,' said Julia.

I felt that I had no choice, so I got up and we left our half-eaten lunches, to walk by the river behind the pub.

'Jim is a strange man,' said Julia as we walked. 'He's his own worst enemy. He isn't strong enough to stop seeing you, so you must do it.'

'But I like spending time with him, and he seems to like me,' I said.

'Ella, I'm asking you to get out of his life. It's very important that you do. If you won't then I will have to take action myself.'

'What do you mean?' I said; the tears were beginning to flow; there was less restraint because there was no-one else around.

'You like being a mediator, don't you?'

'Yes, of course. What has that to do with it?'

'If you don't stop seeing Jim, I'll report you to the panel, so you won't get any more work. Jim was a client; you shouldn't be having a relationship with a client.'

I felt a bit sick. I didn't know whether there was any truth in what she said, but it shocked me. I hadn't thought about the professional implications, and I remembered Chas's warnings and advice. Even if I hadn't done anything actually illegal, I knew that the panel, which decides who gets mediation work, would disapprove. We walked on in silence. I felt that I was between a rock and a hard place.

'I mean it, Ella,' said Julia. 'I'm part of Jim's family now; they've taken me under their wing. I'm not prepared to lose that. There's a lot at stake. I wouldn't be saying this otherwise.'

Julia might look beautiful and confident, but I began to see that she was vulnerable. She needed Jim and his family. Jim didn't need anybody unless they could be useful to him. I suppose that Julia's looks could open doors for him. She was certainly well in with his parents, which was useful to Jim.

'OK, Julia, I'll do what you ask. But I need to tell Jim myself, that's the least I can do.'

'You mustn't tell him about this meeting.'

'Of course not. I'll say that I'm too busy and that I need to focus on my work. In fact, that's true to a point. I have several mediations in the pipeline.'

We walked back along the towpath towards the pub and the car park. There was nothing to say. But when we arrived at her car, Julia said, 'I'm sorry, Ella, but that's how it is.'

I just nodded.

CHAPTER 22
ELLA

I expected Jim to call, since he was hoping for some information about Chas and Alexander. As suggested, he had booked for us to go somewhere special for dinner. For the first time, I didn't have the butterflies in the stomach response when I heard his voice. He must have noticed the change in me. It's surprising what the voice can reveal, especially on the phone.

'Are you OK, Ella? I thought you'd be looking forward to it.'

'Of course I am, I'm just a bit tired. We've got a couple of mediations to prepare for.'

'I hope you're still available for dinner at the end of the week. Are you working with Chas? Don't forget to find out what's the score with Alexander.'

We made our arrangements. When I put the phone down, I felt the need to stand up and walk around. He was as charming as usual, but it wasn't working on me in the same way. I was beginning to see him in a different light. It wasn't a flattering one. I had mixed feelings about our dinner date. One thing I was certain of was that I would not tell tales about Chas. In fact. he had told me about his growing feelings for Alexander and I was pleased for them both.

As usual, I made every effort to look my best for our meeting. He had booked a restaurant that was part of a boutique hotel, so the plan was to spend the night together.

It would probably be the last time, so why not make the most of it? For days and nights, I had considered my way forward. Only one thing was clear to me, I would not ruin my potential career as a mediator. Jim picked me up as usual. He looked especially attractive. I fought down my wave of sadness.

'You look even more gorgeous than usual, Ella. Hard work must agree with you. You really like mediating, don't you?'

'You know, you're spot on. I like it more and more as I get increasing experience.'

'What do you like about it?'

'Getting to understand what makes people behave the way they do. Seeing what's under the tip of the iceberg. It's often quite dark and murky, but fascinating.'

We didn't speak much on the drive. I enjoy being driven by Jim, it's fast and confident. We settled down to our meal. The evening had turned to rain, and it was quite dark outside. In contrast, the small candle-lit tables felt cosy and intimate. It encouraged the conversation.

'Did you find out any more about Chas and Alexander?' he asked.

I took a deep breath. I knew the question had been coming and had rehearsed my answer.

'I am not prepared to spy on Chas. He is a dear friend and colleague and I rely on him. I have to ask you, Jim, what is this thing you have about Alexander? Are you in love with him or what?'

'Don't be ridiculous. Of course not. On the contrary, I dislike him intensely.'

'Why? He apologised to you about the woman who was your girlfriend, paid you £400,000. What more can he do?'

'I'll tell you why I hate him. The woman, as you call her, committed suicide.'

'I am so sorry to hear that, Jim. That's very sad. But I don't understand: what is that to do with Alexander?'

'She was pregnant. Her parents were very strict, found it unacceptable and threw her out.'

'Did she tell him?'

'I don't know. I didn't hear from her, one of her friends contacted me. She took an overdose.'

'That's tragic, I'm so sorry, Jim.'

He took a long drink from his glass of wine. 'I'll never forgive him. She was such a sweet girl.'

I couldn't really think of anything helpful to say, so I just sat quietly. It wasn't easy to move on from that information.

'I waited a long time to get my revenge, but it wasn't really worth the wait. He always gets the better of me, perhaps that's why I can't let it go.'

'I don't think he does it intentionally, Jim. He really is sorry that he took your girlfriend. This isn't helpful to you.'

'What do you mean?'

'This obsession is preventing you from enjoying your life. You have a beautiful girlfriend, a good family; it could be worse, you know.'

Jim poured himself a large drink. 'Let's talk about something else now, shall we?' he said.

I found it hard to think of a new topic of conversation, I was too shocked by what he had told me. Poor Jim, it explained a lot about his behaviour.

'Did anybody else know?' I asked.

'About the suicide?'

'And the pregnancy?'

'She told me that she was pregnant. I was so besotted with her, I offered to marry her. But she said that she didn't want to marry me. That hurt me, I have to say. I couldn't bear to see her after that rejection.'

'Did she tell Alexander that she was pregnant?'

'No, he was away, doing something clever somewhere, South America, I believe. She didn't know where he was or how to contact him. I found out about the suicide from a newspaper some months later.'

'Did you ever think about telling Alexander?'

'I did, but I wanted to have something of her that he didn't. So I decided that it would be my secret. If she'd really wanted him to know, she could have found him, that's what I told myself.'

We managed to make small talk for a while but we both knew that the evening had come to an end. Neither of us felt in the mood for passionate lovemaking. Knowing that it would be the last would have made it too painful for me. I hadn't told Jim about my chat with Julia, but I had decided that I couldn't continue seeing him. Too risky. This wasn't the time to tell him, however.

'I think we both need a quiet time to reflect. I'd like to go home,' I said.

'Of course, Ella. I feel a bit shaken up myself.'

During our return drive, we were both silent. He even drove more slowly. It was as if the wolf was quietly licking his wounds. I saw him brush tears from his eyes. You can't drive fast with tears in your eyes. I put my hand on his leg and gently stroked him, a comfort stroke. He smiled a thank you.

CHAPTER 23
PETER

Roger called me to arrange to meet for a drink. He said he wanted to ask my advice. I agreed to meet him in a pub near where he lived, well away from the House of Commons, for the sake of privacy, he said.

'Thank you for coming, Peter. I guess you're a busy man, so I appreciate it.'

'It's a pleasure, Roger, how are things?'

'I've been thinking about how best to handle my son, Jim. He's not in a good place. Whatever we do, constantly bailing him out and rescuing him, doesn't make any difference. He's as bad as ever. I have an election coming up soon; I don't want him around, he's a loose cannon.'

We had a pint of beer and Roger paused to take a long drink. 'Got any ideas?'

'Perhaps you should stop bailing him out, especially since it seems to have the opposite effect from what you want to achieve. What is that, by the way?'

'We think that it's about time he grew up.'

'Well, he won't, unless he is made to take the consequences for his actions.'

'That could mean prison and disgrace for the family.'

'Do you know why he is behaving in this way? When did it start?'

'After university, when he realised that he wasn't quite as clever as he thought he was. At least, I believe that was the reason.'

'Well, I think that you have to stop rescuing him, for a start.'

We finished our pints and Roger went to the bar to get another round. While he was doing that, I thought about my old friend Chas. He knew a lot about what makes people tick and he'd met Jim in the mediation, so when Roger returned with the beers, I suggested that he have a word with Chas and outlined my reasons for suggesting it.

'Well, I've nothing to lose,' said Roger. 'We just can't go on as we are.'

'It might be a good idea to let Jim know that that you are not going to bail him out any longer.'

'Won't look forward to that discussion,' said Roger. 'But you're right. I have to have it, for everyone's sake.'

'Let me know how you get on. Don't leave it, just do it.'

We finished our drinks and got up to leave.

'Jim is coming round to dinner tomorrow. I'll tell him then. I'll phone you and let you know how it goes.'

'Good luck.'

*

Two days later, Roger phoned me, as promised, to tell me the outcome. The family dinner had started well enough. Jim had invited Julia to join them, and Roger had decided to continue with his plan, believing that Julia's presence might have a positive effect on Jim. When he explained that he wasn't going to go on bailing him out, Jim started shouting and became very upset. Julia tried her best to calm him down, but it didn't have much effect.

'Nobody takes me seriously,' he said.

'How can we when you behave in such an irresponsible way?' was Roger's reply.

'I have made a lot of mistakes in my desire to protect you, Jim. I stayed away from the planning meeting, letting down my constituents, just to get the developers off your back. No more. I will have to work extra hard now if I don't want to lose my seat. I realise that I like being an MP and try to do a good job. Your behaviour is putting that at risk. Sorry to have to say this, but it's about time you grew up.'

Jim looked stunned. His father had never spoken like that to him before, which made it all the more powerful.

'I thought he was going to storm out,' Roger told me. 'Instead, he started to cry.'

Nobody could eat any more of their dinner. They just sat there and looked at Jim.

'It was awful,' explained Roger.

I reassured him that it had been necessary, and that Jim would get over it.

'Well done,' I said. 'I know it must have been difficult, to say the least.'

*

The next day I had another call from Roger.

'I'm a bit worried about Jim, he's gone missing.'

'Perhaps he needed a bit of a cooling off period,' I said.

'Could you have a word with that mediator chap, Chas? He's more used to this emotional stuff, he knows quite a bit about Jim. See what he thinks?'

'I'll do my best, Roger. I know he's pretty busy right now, but I'll give him a call.'

Chas has put a lot of work my way lately and I don't want to give him any hassle. On the other hand, Roger is a good man who needs all the support he can get, so I found time to give Chas a call and put him in the picture.

'Just give me a few days to work out how best to help,' was his response.

I felt that was the best I could do.

CHAPTER 24
ELLA

Chas called me to set up a meeting with him. He wanted to discuss something important, he said. He wouldn't say any more. It all sounded a bit mysterious, very unlike Chas. He might be like a cat in some ways but he's usually very straight about work matters. I assumed it was about work. I was wrong, or at least partly wrong.

We met in the coffee shop with the wallpaper like shelves of books. It was as if we were having our meeting in a library or a study. The leather armchairs and squashy sofas added to the impression, and unusually we had the place to ourselves, no mums with small children. He ordered our coffees and took a file out of his briefcase.

'Ella, I know this might be difficult for you, but I want to talk to you about Jim.'

I delayed picking up my cup of coffee just in case I spilt it.

'Jim is at a sort of crossroads. His father has decided that it's time he grew up. He's withdrawing financial support and told Jim that it's about time he took responsibility for his life.'

I just sat quietly, looking at Chas, trying to work out the implications of this bombshell, which is how it must have felt to Jim.

'Jim doesn't need the financial support at the moment. He's just had £400,000 from Alexander. But the way he behaves, that will soon be gone. He probably owes quite a lot of it already,' said Chas.

I felt sure that he was right. The way Jim spent money was awesome, he seemed to have no idea of how to manage it. Or else he was making a statement.

'It's not just the money,' I said. 'Jim needs his family. He's a very angry man and a vulnerable one.'

'You're right, Ella. There's something bugging him, eating away at him, causing his bad behaviour. Do you have any idea of what it might be?'

I now felt steady enough to sip my coffee.

'Yes, he told me, but I assume it was in confidence. All I can say is that it goes back to his time in university and that trouble with Alexander.'

'I thought so. I know that Alexander is finding Jim's behaviour upsetting. For everyone's sake something needs to be done.'

I nodded my head in agreement. 'But what, Chas?'

'I have an idea, Ella, but it means you have to challenge yourself. It might be distressing for you.'

'Go on, tell me. I trust you, Chas.'

'A mediation is in order here, between Jim and Alexander.'

I felt my heart rate speed up, and it wasn't due to the caffeine.

'I want you to be the mediator, Ella. I know it breaks the rules, but this will be an informal meeting, facilitated by you.'

'Why not you, Chas?'

'I just know it will work better with you. Are you up for it? It is the greatest gift you can give Jim, if you feel able to do it.'

'I just need to think about it. Give me twenty-four hours.'

'Fair enough. Thank you, let's speak tomorrow.'

He put the papers back into his briefcase and stood up to leave.

'By the way, there will be no papers to read, just some feelings to get to the bottom of. I think you can do it.'

He smiled his Cheshire cat smile and left me with my cold cup of coffee.

I spent the rest of the day and evening thinking about Jim and the idea of a mediation. The more I thought about it the better I liked it. It would be difficult for all of us, including me. But I loved Jim enough to give it a try. I knew he didn't love me and if I could help him, at least we should be able to be friends. Because it is informal, as it were, I wouldn't be able to put the mediation on my CV. So what, Chas will know about it. It must have been the right decision, because I slept well.

*

The next morning, I phoned Chas.

'OK, Chas, I'll do it. On one condition. I want you there with me. Who will set it up?'

'I've spoken to Alexander, and he has agreed, and Jim's father will tell him that any further support of any kind will be conditional on him agreeing to this mediation.'

'It's not a good start when the parties aren't too keen on mediation.'

'I know that, Ella, but the end may justify the means in this case. I'll suggest a day next week and make some rooms in my chambers available.'

So that was it. It was going to happen.

CHAPTER 25
ELLA

It seemed strange preparing for a mediation with no documents to pore over to try to get to grips with the details of the dispute. Not necessary in this case. I knew all that I needed to know. At least I thought I did. As usual, I didn't fancy breakfast and began to feel butterflies in my stomach as I thought about the morning ahead. I dressed with the same care as if it was the usual sort of mediation with strangers and their lawyers, making sure to wear my lucky silver earrings.

When I got to Chas's chambers, he was already there. His usual cat-like poise seemed a bit more ruffled than usual. I know that he was in love with Alexander and was nervous on his behalf. Strangely my nervousness had evaporated, replaced by anticipation. I relished the idea of being able to help someone I loved move on to a better place. There was no doubt in my mind that choosing my career over Jim was the right decision. So now was my chance to prove it. I didn't quite know who to, perhaps to myself.

Jim turned up first. We greeted each other formally. He looked subdued, but his chin had that determined thrust to it. He was lovely to look at. Then Alexander arrived. He and Chas shared glances, Chas was the more nervous. I resolved to do my best for these people who meant such a lot to me.

'Let's make a start,' I said. Not too cheerful but sounding positive.

We sat around an oval table, with Jim and Alexander at opposite ends as far apart as possible. Chas and I occupied the seats between them. I began with the usual introductions about confidentiality, and told them that they can stop the process if they want to, adding that I hope that they don't do that. They have been in this situation before, so they know the drill.

I asked Jim if he'd like to make an opening statement, hoping that he could stay calm and not lose his temper.

Jim cleared his throat. He had no notes. I could see that he intended to tell it how he sees it. Alexander and Chas gave him their whole attention.

'Do you remember Angela?' he said, looking at Alexander. 'She was my girlfriend until you came along and enticed her away.'

Alexander opened his mouth to say something, but after a hard look from Chas, he closed it again.

'You didn't really want her, did you? You just toyed with her for a while and then you dumped her. I loved her but she wouldn't look at me after she had been with you. Because you were so much smarter and cleverer than me. I was lost without her. But that's not the end of it. She committed suicide; did you know that?'

We could all see from the shock on Alexander's face that he didn't know.

'I'm so sorry,' he said.

'You bloody well should be,' said Jim. 'She was pregnant. Being an unmarried mother was too much to take, so she took pills and killed herself. I hope you can live with that. I find it difficult enough and it wasn't me that made her pregnant. I'll never forgive you.'

The outburst seemed to have exhausted Jim and he slumped down in his chair. We all sat quietly for a while. Then I asked Alexander if he wanted to make any comments or ask any questions. He nodded his reply.

'First of all, I would like to say how sorry I am, Jim. Angela was a lovely girl, but an angel she wasn't. I took her home on the evening we met because you were too drunk to drive, and she asked me to. I was at that time exploring my own sexuality, beginning to realise that I might be gay. Angela was very attractive. We went around together for a while, but we never had sex. I have never been sexually interested in women. She was having plenty of sex, so she told me, but I can assure you that it was never with me. Whoever got her pregnant, it wasn't me. I'm very sorry to hear about the suicide. If she had told me she was pregnant, I would have done what I could to help even though I wasn't the one who made her pregnant.'

Jim sat up straight as Alexander explained his part, or non-part, in Angela's sad life. He looked at Alexander and could see that he was telling the truth.

'So why did you feel so guilty if you didn't really do anything?'

'I know that I didn't behave well. You see, I used Angela to hide my homosexuality. She wasn't the only one. Women have always been attracted to me. I don't really know why. Perhaps it's because deep down they know that they are safe with me. I used that to protect myself. It took me a long time to accept that I'm gay.'

I could see Chas looking at him with great pride and affection.

'Jim, do you want to make a comment or ask Alexander any questions?' I prompted.

'No, I just need time to get my head around it all,' he said.

I was reminded of a comment in a book by Graham Greene.

Those who thought, forgot, those who felt, remembered, was the gist of it. It explained the difference between Jim and Alexander. Jim felt, Alexander thought.

I suggested that we took a break for coffee and biscuits. My lack of breakfast and high-energy input was beginning to tell. I also wanted a quiet word with Chas. Coffee was brought in and Jim and Alexander stayed where they were while Chas and I went outside the room.

'Well done, Ella,' he said. 'What revelations. Did you know all that?'

'No, but it explains a lot. How do you think we should proceed?'

'Alexander has apologised. Do you think Jim would be able to do the same? Why don't you take him aside and ask him, Ella? I think he would accept it from you.'

I went back into the room and asked Jim to come and have a word with me.

'Jim, I know you are a proud man. For the sake of your family and Julia, you need to get shot of all this. Saying sorry can be a way of doing that. Do you think you could, please?'

He said nothing for what seemed like a long time. Then he looked at me. There were tears in his eyes.

'I'll do it, Ella, for you. And because I know you're right.'

I smiled and held his hand for moment. Then I let him go.

The four of us sat around the table again. The atmosphere felt lighter although still serious.

'I just want to say sorry, Alexander,' Jim said in a small voice.

Alexander stood up and walked around the table towards Jim.

'Let's just shake hands, Jim,' he said and held out his hand.

Jim took his hand and pulled him into a rough hug. Chas and I just looked at each other. I had to blink back my tears.

*

That evening, I got a phone call from Chas. I was sipping a glass of Muscadet.

'Ella, well done! You really are a star mediator, I'm proud of you. What are you thinking now?'

'About the tip of the iceberg,' I said.

'Indeed,' replied Chas.

'And all the interesting stuff beneath it.'

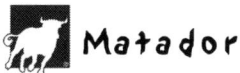

For exclusive discounts on Matador titles,
sign up to our occasional newsletter at
troubador.co.uk/bookshop